The Daughter of the Hawk

The Daughter of the Hawk

by

C. S. FORESTER

Author of Love Lies Dreaming
One Wonderful Week

THE BOBBS-MERRILL COMPANY
PUBLISHERS   INDIANAPOLIS

The Daughter of the Hawk

The Daughter of the Hawk

CHAPTER I

THIS book is not going to be written about the Hawk, *El Halcón Real*—Hawk Royal —but one can hardly help mentioning him without plunging into further detail about him. Perhaps one day when the *Encyclopœdia Britannica* is again revised it will include two lines about him; not, of course, under the heading "Royle, Francis John"—he is not important enough for that—but he may be mentioned parenthetically under the heading "History" in the article dealing with the Rainless Republic under the equator where he died.

He was a little man, fierce and frail as a flame, and men loved him. After the war he was Major Royle, late R.E., but he was not a professional soldier. He was a miner, and he had owned and managed a silver mine in the Andean foot-hills in

7

the Rainless Republic before the war. After the war, and after the death of his young wife, he had left his little daughter in the charge of relatives and had gone back to the Rainless Coast. There he had found that the few vague and unsatisfactory letters he had received from his Spanish-American agent had told part of the truth. Five years is a long time in the life of a South American republic, especially when the grandmotherly supervision of the United States is distracted by a European war. A certain Señor Eguia, who had once been an entirely undistinguished lawyer on the Rainless Coast, had suddenly developed into a politician and then (it is a not unusual transition for a Spanish-American lawyer) into a militant statesman. Unexpectedly, he had proved more cunning, more truculent, more unsparingly bloodthirsty than his rivals, and after quite a small revolution and a few hundred perfectly legal executions he had ascended the presidential chair in the same week that Major Royle had earned the D.S.O. for his determined gallantry in destroying a bridge over the Aisne under heavy fire during the German offensive in 1918.

Señor Eguia took prompt measures for the replenishment of the public treasury and of his private savings, making the most of the time allotted him during the preoccupation of the Great Powers. By methods entirely constitutional he had killed off the rich men of the Republic, and confiscated their estates. He cast a covetous eye upon Major Royle's silver mine,—the only mine of any sort throughout the length and breadth of that most distressful country,—and what Eguia coveted he obtained. Silver had soared to an amazing price now that gold had disappeared, and the produce of the mine would give Eguia the money he needed to pay his soldiers and to build the little fleet for which he yearned; it would give him part of the constant revenue which all South American potentates find so necessary and unobtainable. A senatorial decree (Eguia governed by means of senatorial decrees, which were legal and readily obtained) announced that the produce of the soil was inherently the property of the government. Another declared that the concession granted to Royle by Eguia's predecessor's predecessor, whose throat had long ago been cut by his negro guards, was unconstitutional and void from the first. Eguia quietly gained possession of Royle's mine.

Such was the state of affairs which Royle had found when he arrived on the Rainless Coast. The work to which he had devoted so much of his fierce energy, and on which he had steadily lavished all its increasing returns, was reft from him. The roads he had blasted through the Andean rocks, the peons he had trained to labor, the plant he had transported thither on muleback at such appalling cost were all of them in the hands of Eguia and his sallow-skinned henchmen. Royle was nonchalantly informed of the fact, and his expostulations were pointedly countered by his arrest and deportation as an undesirable alien. Perhaps Eguia thought then that he was rid of him; perhaps he did not reckon on Royle's reckless pugnacity; perhaps he did not care.

However it was, no sooner had Royle disembarked in the neighboring republic, two hundred miles down the coast, than he turned back, bent either on regaining his own or on taking revenge. Here and there, almost moneyless though he was, he picked up recruits. (Dawkins, the man about whom this book is to be written, joined him later.) Then, careless of the odds against him, he flung a challenge at Eguia and appeared in the Rainless

Republic, a rebel, a filibuster, a disturber of the established order.

Whether or not the tale of those two bloody years will ever be told is more than man can guess —if by "told" is implied its publication in the civilization of the West. For on the Rainless Coast it is told a thousand times. The Indians of the Cordilleras tell it in the evenings, crouching round their fires in the piercing Andean cold, helping out their limited vocabulary with gesture and pantomime; the lovelorn youths of the cities, wailing their unrequited passions under curtained windows, drag mentions of the Hawk into their limping verses. For Royle became the Hawk, and perhaps by a simple translation of his name, he became *El Halcón Real,* Hawk Royal. It was his fierce swoops down from his mountain fastnesses which won him his name. The presidential troops wore themselves to rags in desperate marches and countermarches after him, but they could not catch him. Sometimes he had a bare dozen of men with him, sometimes as many as five hundred. With them he set Eguia's dictatorship at defiance, and kept all the Rainless Republic in a state of turmoil. Anywhere within ten degrees of the equator you can hear tales of his reckless, insane valor. Some of them, as has been hinted, have already made their way into verse, and perhaps a century hence will witness the blossoming of some new Iliad or Odyssey which will represent the blending of these embryo sagas and will recount the bloody history of the rivalry between Hawk Royal and El Presidente Eguia.

Men thought he was more than human, although they loved him. Eguia's press said he was mad, and that might pehaps be nearer the truth; for the death of his young wife may have brought him the happy madness of not caring whether he lived or died. Twice he had eluded pursuing regiments, and, pelting into the coastal plain with his shoeless followers, he had borne panic into the streets of Bolivar itself, and the government had tottered almost to destruction before desperate forced marches had brought up sufficient regular troops to bar even his path. He had established a navy of canoes on the long lake between the Cordilleras and had thereby given a most instructive demonstration of the efficiency and the limitations of sea power. His men went unpaid and almost unfed, for the most part, but the magic of his personality and his marvelous energy succeeded in keeping a faithful few round him.

An early recruit was Henry Dawkins, Englishman and loafer, with the usual doubtful past and more than doubtful future. Dawkins held by him to the end, acting as vice-admiral of the dugout navy and as lieutenant-general of the shoeless army, serving his chief with a steady devotion surprising in a man of his antecedents—although not at all surprising to one who had been in contact with the Hawk's personality.

Royle's success could not last. He had taken every chance Fate offered him. A dozen times he had faced situations wherein the odds against his coming through were at least a hundred to one, and each time he had emerged with his life and with some of his ragged regiment at his back. But Eguia fought him with savage energy, and Eguia had the power of the long purse. The end of the European war and the topsyturvydom of the European exchanges made it possible for him to buy all the arms and ammunition he needed, and to officer his straggling battalions with hard-bitten

German infantry majors. A steel motor-boat armed with machine-guns, borne in sections with infinite labor over the foot-hills of the Cordilleras, swept the Hawk's dugout navy from the lake, and his conscript battalions held furiously on to the Hawk's trail along the Andean snow-line, while the German officers saw to it that never again could the Hawk have a chance of surprising his pursuers, as he had done so often before, and of driving ten times his strength before him with many invaluable captures of rifles and cartridges. Turn and double as he might, there was always some hard-marching brigade at his heels. His tiny army, with never a chance of plundering for food, fell piece-meal into the pursuer's hands. At first they were crucified or hanged or burned alive, according to Eguia's whim at the moment, but later they were not killed out of hand; Eguia had found another use for them.

The end came after one last spattering skirmish. A bullet pierced the Hawk's foot, and although the faithful Dawkins got him away the few survivors of the battle dropped away from them during the night. Dawkins and the Hawk, on overdriven mules, eluded pursuit for days, starving in the piercing cold. Gangrene appeared in the Hawk's wound. He died, a merciful death, in Dawkins' arms even as the inexorable pursuers came in sight again across the limitless hills. But Dawkins, they spared, because Eguia had issued orders that he wanted prisoners—healthy, able-bodied prisoners.

CHAPTER II

PERHAPS Eguia had not really intended to spare the Englishman, Henry Dawkins, for he had been the Hawk's right hand for eighteen bloody months. Nevertheless, when at last the news reached him that the Hawk was dead and Dawkins a captive, Eguia relented, for his own purposes, and suffered him to live, for Dawkins had inspired no devotion and was the hero of no budding legends. Besides, Dawkins was a man of powerful build, heavy-shouldered and ample-thighed, and Eguia had need of men like that.

To explain this need of Eguia calls for a further excursion into history, and into geological history as well as political history. Off the Rainless Coast of South America lies a number of little islands, as rainless as the coast they neighbor. The sea that surrounds them is full of fish; there is, and seemingly always has been, an inexhaustible supply of fish in the American Pacific. The islands have in consequence been the resort of uncounted millions of sea-birds during uncounted centuries, uncounted thousands of years, even. In the absence of rain the islands were in consequence coated thick with guano. During the 'fifties and 'sixties and 'seventies of last century, and since then to a less extent the guano was dug off the islands and brought to Europe round the Horn in the big wind-jammers. Fortunes were made from guano, and little wars were fought between South American states to determine possession of some of the guano islands. Previously no one had bothered about who owned these tiny fragments of arid land.

Birds Island (to this day there is a doubt as to whether there should or should not be an apostrophe in the name; whether it derives from its myriads of sea-birds or from Bird, the Pacific buccaneer) did not quite come into the same category. It was a well-known and charted island, fifty miles from the Rainless Coast, and the guano prospectors had early visited it. But their report was unfavorable—the guano was not thick enough to make its collection profitable. Nevertheless, the prospectors had missed a huge prize, for they had not bothered to examine what lay beneath the guano.

At some time or other, some centuries ago, a submarine earthquake had sunk Birds Island below the sea, along with its cap of guano, and after just the right interval (the geologists are in doubt as to whether this would be fifty or five hundred years) another disturbance had cast it to the surface again. The guano cap had been converted into one huge chunk of pure phosphate, much more valuable than mere guano, more valuable even than the nitrate fields on the mainland for which Chile and Peru had fought their desperate war in the 'eighties. Since the second upheaval just sufficient guano had been deposited to conceal from casual inspection the value of what lay beneath. Of late more than one of these islands have been proved to be what they are. Birds Island is the most recent of them, and the discovery occurred just when Eguia's battalions were trampling out the last embers of the rebellion kindled by the Hawk.

The island was part of the Rainless Republic—her neighbors who had idly let it fall into her hands long ago gnashed their teeth now at the news—and Eguia did in part what was expected of him. He deeded the island, in his presidential capacity, to himself in his private capacity. That was only natural and inevitable, but his next step was more unusual. Any ordinary president would have promptly sold his concession to an American or European syndicate, accepting half its value for a quick sale, but Eguia was of sterner stuff, while money was "tight" in all the markets. Eguia saw himself in possession of endless supplies of unpaid labor, and he proposed to work the island himself. General Aranguren, the least intelligent of his officials, was appointed governor of Birds Island and sent thither with half a battalion. The Navy (two obsolete torpedo-gunboats) brought him cargoes of stores—a distilling plant, for the island was of course waterless, and adobe bricks, and timber in small quantity, and endless supplies of sacking. The general was instructed to build a house for himself, another for his officers, some sort of compound for the men, and another—here Eguia disclosed his plan for the first time—for the convicts. And as soon as this was done (it did not take long) the Navy began to bring over living cargoes. Some two hundred convicts, dragged from the filthy prisons at Bolivar and elsewhere, composed the first batch. Ten of them were women. Eguia's orders commanded him to set the women to stitching sacks while the men shoveled the island piecemeal into them. President Eguia went on to say what he considered the minimum task for a man or a woman. It was hardly necessary for him to say what would happen to the general if the convicts did not complete their daily quota. Other necessary work, such as building a jetty out on the eastern side of the island, where there was a channel through the coral barrier, was thrown in, in addition. Eguia was using the state prisoners to dig his phosphate for him, the Army to guard it, the Navy to transport it, all without cost to himself; disinterested observers said that Eguia was "on a good thing."

And Eguia saw no reason to soften the lot of those he sent to Birds Island. The monstrous task of filling and of carrying down to the jetty nineteen sacks of phosphate a day was imposed upon every male convict; and to each of the ten wretched women, who were penned off in a separate tiny compound, was given the task of daily providing the sacks used by nineteen men—three hundred sixty-one per day, in other words. Eguia did not rob the State unduly. It was put to little expense in the matter of food for the prisoners; and housing, in that climate, cost next to nothing—adobe walls and a few miles of barbed wire housed them satisfactorily enough.

But prison diet and distilled water and over-heavy labor and the monstrous cruelties of the guards combined to create a constant demand for fresh labor. Lucky convicts died after a fortnight on Birds Island; hardy ones survived for almost a year, if they did not develop the dreadful sores which the raw phosphate caused in some subjects. Justice was in consequence administered throughout the Rainless Republic with a strictness hitherto unknown—an all-embracing strictness, in fact. No one was ever tried nowadays without conviction, and conviction always carried with it a sentence of hard labor. Eguia saw to that in his instructions to his judges. But the Rainless Republic is small, and its population scanty. The supply of convicts hardly satisfied the demand. That was why Eguia's officers' eyes brightened when they looked at Henry Dawkins' big shoulders, and the hard-bitten strength of his muscles.

CHAPTER III

THE chain-gangs were setting out on their afternoon's work at the close of the siesta. Fifty shabby soldiers were drawn up in line at the exit to the barbed-wire compound, and the adobe machine-gun tower outside one of its angles was fully manned. When twenty men had passed the first barrier the sergeant in command of the gate screamed out an order, and the sluggish tide of sulky prisoners eddied back, while the twenty men were harnessed, with the rapidity of long practise, into their equipment. This consisted of a very long chain, to which at regular intervals were attached twenty pairs of shorter chains. One of each short pair was passed round the waist of the prisoner, pulled as tight as might be, and padlocked into position. To the corresponding short chains were permanently attached, alternately, a spade or a pickax. When a gang of twenty had thus been locked together two soldiers took command of it, at whose orders the chain-gang loaded themselves with sacks from a pile at hand, shouldered their tools, and marched clanking out of the second barrier up the slope to begin their work.

The fourth chain-gang was the usual motley mixture. There were Spanish-Americans of all possible mixtures of blood: European, Indian and negro. One and all were lean and wolfish, and for the most part they were dressed in tattered shirts and drawers although a negro at the tail of the line was completely naked. Through the holes in their clothes could be seen long thick scars, varying in color from red to white, whose origin clearly lay in the *látigo,* the mule-whip, which trailed in the hand of the corporal in command. A fair proportion displayed the running angry sores which the phosphate caused in some subjects. Heads down, spiritless and starving, their chains beating a dreary time to their step, they marched under the changeless turquoise sky over the tumbled dusty earth.

For on Birds Island there was not a blade of vegetation. It was just a vast rounded hummock of phosphate-covered rock protruding from the sea. At its westerly side it was cut into a steep cliff by the eternal Pacific swell, which broke in a continual recurrent thunder against it—a thunder which to the newcomers was the most noticeable noise in the island, but which was so steady and monotonous as to strike unheeded the ears of those who had been there for any length of time. Overhead and out over the blue sea wheeled clouds of sea-birds, white gannets and white gulls, black-and-white gulls, gray-and-white gulls, screaming in their high piping voices, with an occasional frigate-bird with his terrible red beak or an albatross soaring on motionless wings. One noticed the cry of the gulls however long one was on Birds Island, perhaps because it was variable, and because it ceased at night.

The fifth in the line of the fourth chain-gang was of a different type from the others. He was a much larger man, with a great spread and thickness to his shoulders. He was more of a blond, with a mat of tangled golden-brown hair and a heavy tawny beard and mustache, in contrast with the straggling black growths of his fellows. His eyes were blue-gray, and, although they scowled and were drawn narrow as though with continual fretting, their expression was not cowed and fright-

ened and sidelong, as was that of the dark eyes of
the others. His arms, tanned to a deep brown, ex-
hibited a definition and a sharpness of muscle due
to continual heavy work. Biceps and triceps in the
upper arm, the digitations of the flexors and ex-
tensors in the forearm were all clear and defined,
unmasked by subcutaneous fat or rudimentary hair
growth. With his magnificent muscular development and his scowling, narrow forehead he looked,
as he tramped sullenly along, pickax on shoulder,
like some living bronze replica of Rodin's *Thinker*.
Where neck and shoulder met was an angry red
stripe blotched with blackened blood, an unfailing
lure to a host of flies; the gang-corporal had been
bad tempered that morning.

Life on Birds Island was absurdly simple, as
simple as Eguia's well-thought-out regulations
could make it. Twenty men chained together can
not hope to rebel successfully—a bullet or two
sent into the mass of them would cumber them
with corpses even if they could all resolve to act
together. Their very pickaxes and spades were
chained to them on a four-foot chain which did
not hamper their digging, but made it impossible
(as had occurred before the innovation was made)

for a desperate man to fling his tool at a guard and earn the summary execution which would end his troubles.

The fourth gang proceeded according to rule. It marched to its allocated area, extended in line at the point where it had left off that morning, laid down its sacks and began to dig. The shovel men rested on their spades; the pickax men swung their picks stolidly, breaking up the soil. For the first few inches the work was easy, but lower down the phosphate was almost flintlike in its hardness, and the picks struck against it with a hard metallic clatter which was audible from a considerable distance. For ten minutes the noise went on, the clash and thump of the picks, the grunts and heavy breathing of the workers, and as the pace inevitably slackened, the zip-crack of the *látigo* wielded by the gang-corporal. But when this latter official decided that enough had been broken up a curt order ended the pickax men's labor for the time. All they had to do next was to hold open the sacks while the shovel men filled them with the broken soil. Then, when all the fragments were cleared off, they fell to their pick work again.

From this it will seem obvious that the spade

men had the easier task, and so it was. That was why the sergeant at the gate had to have a long memory, because he had to see that a man who wielded a pick one day wielded a shovel the next —unless the sergeant took a dislike to a man and caused him to be put on pick work out of his turn.

Pick succeeded shovel and shovel succeeded pick until the sacks were full, and then both sections enjoyed a change of task. At a command from the corporal each man endeavored and succeeded, after a struggle, to hoist a full sack upon his shoulders. Thus they marched the half-mile down to the jetty, each man staggering and gasping under his load of one hundred and fifty pounds of phosphate. They picked their steps with care, for were a man to stumble or fall, chained as he was to his companions, the latter might be pulled off their feet also; it was not unknown for the whole overburdened twenty to be dragged to the ground together, with sacks rolling hither and thither, and the exasperated gang-corporal's *látigo* taking off flakes of skin from all and sundry.

It would, of course, have been easy for Eguia to supply some kind of light railway with hand trucks to lessen this labor, and any ordinary em-

ployer would have found that it paid to do so; but
not so Eguia. He paid absolutely nothing for his
labor, so that it was bound to be cheaper to use
men instead of machines. Nineteen sacks a day
was the daily amount Eguia demanded per man, so
that nineteen times a day each man carried a full
sack some half-mile to the jetty and marched the
half-mile back—nine and a half miles loaded and
nine and a half miles light, besides the digging.
Eguia's estimate of the maximum to be demanded
of a man was a very close one, even if a trifle
exaggerated.

It was a dreary monotonous life on Birds Island.
Dig, dig, dig, shovel, shovel, shovel, carry sacks,
feed (lightly), sleep like animals, and start again
next day. Every few days would come a slight
change for some of them when the cargo lighters
had to be filled for the loading of the ships, but
that was the only source of variety—that and the
gang-corporal's *látigo*. Sometimes the sky would
change from its usual polished turquoise to a
shade of deeper blue; sometimes white clouds,
even, would throng up from the horizon; for five
minutes every six months it would even rain
slightly. Through it all, hour by hour, the great

Pacific swell would break, at ninety-second intervals, against the cliffs to the westward, and during the hours of daylight the gulls kept up their monotonous piping—but the gulls were gradually leaving the place now that men had established themselves there. Birds Island would soon be silent save for the surf and the din of men's labor.

The guards were as unhappy—almost—as the prisoners. The monotony of their existence palled eventually even upon such minds as they possessed, despite the fact of occasional distractions—issues of ardent spirits and regular permits to enter the women's compound. For the female prisoners, as was only to be expected, did double duty; they made sacks by day and rejoiced the hearts of the soldiers by night, although, prematurely aged and hideous as they were, bowed, toothless and scarred, they hardly seemed especially adapted for this latter function. Most of the soldiers, inevitably, cast longing eyes upon the officers' wives and their maids, in the gleaming, whitewashed, adobe buildings beyond the jetty.

So that it is easy to think of possible reasons for the ill temper of Corporal Barroso, in command of the fourth chain-gang, and why his eyes flashed viciously at his laboring slaves, and why he snarled his orders with a gleam of white teeth under his black mustache, and why his *látigo* bit so deep into the wincing flesh of the pickax men.

Henry Dawkins suffered Barroso's little attentions mutely. A year of Birds Island had taught him to hold back his fierce temper with a large hand. A gang-corporal with a sense of humor could enliven a whole day by goading a desperate convict with jeers and lashes, and could find huge delight in his victim's cries and grimaces. With luck he might even stimulate him into open mutiny, resulting, of course, in a full-dress flogging— one hundred lashes before the assembled convicts and probable resultant death from gangrene or shock. Henry Dawkins was one of the few men on the island who had survived even fifty lashes (his back was corrugated, criss-cross, with the white scars of them), and he had no intention of suffering that again. He did what he could to keep the corporal's attention from him: he worked really hard; he picked his steps carefully when marching back loaded (hitching the sack to his other shoulder so that the coarse sacking and the lumps inside would not chafe his new wound) and never by look or by gesture did he let Barroso know how he was fuming internally. He flung his pick into the ringing soil with a fierce effort; he wrenched the point loose, swung it up again, and brought it down once more—hips, thighs, shoulders and arms all working in unison and contributing their share of the labor; to the eye of a sculptor or an artist the rippling play of the muscles under the skin would have been sheer joy. Corporal Barroso noticed nothing to grow enthusiastic about.

Dully through Dawkins' mind passed his usual train of thought as he swung his pick—the same old thoughts drifting backward and forward without progress like a tiger in a cage. He was glad the Hawk had never lived to suffer this, for he had loved the Hawk. And the Hawk would never have borne forced labor; he would have refused from the first and died, dumb-mad, at the flogging triangles. His slim white body would have been slashed and torn by the whips of plaited hide, while the sergeants stood round and grinned at the spectacle. Better was it that he had died of starvation and gangrene in the Cordilleras. Henry Dawkins came to the same conclusion twice an hour, every day at Birds Island, but he found no comfort in it.

Then his thoughts drifted on, to the weariness of his muscles, the foulness of the food he had eaten, to the possibility of making his way, some moonless night, through the barbed wire of the enclosure, past the sentries, to the motor-boat at the jetty and freedom. Henry Dawkins knew the fate of those who had tried. He decided, for the thousandth time, not to make the attempt until chance made the possibilities more favorable—or until he could bear his life no longer. He sent his pick crashing into the stony phosphate with desperate venom.

It was then that Henry Dawkins noticed something unusual about the soil he was digging. He was turning up big oblong lumps of a size and shape he was not used to, and of a white color as distinct from the grayish-brown phosphate. And these lumps were heavy, and his pick rang against them with a more metallic sound than was quite natural. At his next blow the white coating of a lump flaked away, revealing a white metallic luster. Dawkins checked in his swing in surprise. He stooped and looked. Lead? Perhaps—but most likely silver! His frantic gesticulation actually had the effect of arresting Corporal Barroso's arm in mid-air so that the *látigo* caressed his shoulder rather than cut it again. Dawkins picked up the lump; surely enough it was an ingot of silver, and there were half a dozen others lying at his feet. They were coated with a thin layer of silver phosphate, as a result of much time in that soil, but there was no doubting their value. The one word "silver" had the effect of calming Barroso's fiendish rage at the delay, and it sped back and forth in an excited buzz along the chain-gang. Barroso took the ingot in his hands, and his expression changed to one of desperate greed. His surprise had been great enough to carry him momentarily within range of the picks and shovels of half a dozen of the gang, although he backed away at once as soon as he remembered.

"More?" he demanded, and Dawkins handed over to him the four or five ingots he had turned up. Corporal Barroso piled them before him, and motioned to Dawkins to go on digging. So Dawkins' pick swung up and down again, up and down, and at every few strokes the spadesmen at his left or right stooped hurriedly and pulled from the deepening hole a fresh lump of silver. The other members of the gang stood idle, staring

fascinated at the treasure which was being un-
earthed before their eyes, and even Barroso forgot
to order them to recommence digging.

Up and down went Dawkins' pick, and ingot
after ingot was lifted from the hole. Suddenly
the note of the pick upon the ground changed
somewhat, and at the next stroke a splintering
crash was heard and the pick head half buried itself unexpectedly. Dawkins wrenched it free, and
he and Barroso stooped to look. The rest of the
gang tried to gather round, gesticulating and chattering in amazement, but Barroso turned on them
with a snarl and drove them back, and a sharp
order to the dumfounded private of the guard
close at hand saw to it that they would not be permitted to approach again. The spadesmen on
Dawkins' left and right cleared away the debris,
cautiously, and once more Dawkins brought down
his pick with a shattering crash. At this low level
a big iron-bound chest had once been sunk, but
the passage of centuries had eaten away both iron
and wood, and it was only a thin weakly shell
which Dawkins' pick smashed into fragments.

But the chest had held good up till then, had
prevented the phosphate from tarnishing the con-

tents. The sun was reflected, dazzlingly, from a thousand surfaces of bright gold. Gold coins there were, any number of them, massed in one compartment of the chest. The other half of the chest was full of gold plate—chalices, pyxes, crucifixes, the plunder seemingly of a dozen of the cathedrals of the mainland in the days when El Dorado was not obviously a wild fragment of a dream. At the spectacle even Barroso forgot the need to keep himself out of reach of the gang; he sprang forward and knelt grotesquely in the hole on the lumps of phosphate; he plunged his hands greedily in the heap of coins; he picked up and turned forward and back a broad gold pyx which reflected the sunlight in a wide arc of ruddy gold. He uttered broken, loving foolishnesses as he caressed this mass of wealth. A heavy gold reliquary, gaudily carved and enameled, came into his hands, and emitted a curious stony chink as he turned it over —a sound which has no counterpart on earth. He fumbled it open; it was the size and much the shape of a long flat pencil box. As the lid lifted the sun was reflected in a new fashion and from a thousand new facets, for the box was filled with precious stones.

Dawkins' startled eyes gaped at this new wonder as he bent over Barroso's kneeling form. Dawkins was the unworthy scion of a younger branch of the great Dawkins family of pawnbrokers; he had been in the business himself before the untimely incident which had driven him hurriedly to South America. He knew, as he peered into the box, that he was gazing at the equivalent of scores of thousands of pounds. Diamonds were there, mostly cut but many of them uncut. There were big, milky white pearls there in dozens. Here and there was the red fire of a ruby, or the calm green of an emerald. But most of the stones were diamonds, big white glittering diamonds, and with the trembling of Barroso's hands the sunlight shot hither and thither from the facets with a shimmering sparkle which held Dawkins fascinated.

It was in fact Barroso who roused himself first. With a wild effort he pulled himself upright and stepped backward out of the hole, the box still in his hands. He faced the chain-gang with a snarl, and he glowered sidelong at the stupid private who stood rifle in hand at his elbow. To Dawkins it was obvious that his mind was working furiously, and immediately it was just as obvious that he had hit on a plan.

"Go fetch the captain," snapped Barroso to the private.

"The captain?" repeated the private, stupid as ever.

"Yes, fool. El Capitan Vergara. Who else? Go, you fool! Run!"

The private hastened off at a shambling trot. Barroso closed the reliquary, put it beneath his arm, and seized and cocked his rifle with obvious menace.

"About turn," said he to the gang, and they obeyed, helpless as ever.

"March!" he said; then, when they had gone a dozen paces, "Halt!"

To the dull minds of the chain-gang this might have seemed a mere precaution to keep them away from the treasure, but Dawkins' straining ears (he dared not turn to look) caught the sound of the box being reopened; he heard the stones cascade out of the box—into Barroso's pocket, he shrewdly guessed—and he heard the box closed again. Minute by minute passed. Some one in the gang stirred uneasily, and tried to turn, but a fierce growl from Barroso froze him stiff again. The gang stood patiently still, with the sun beating into their eyes.

Then Dawkins heard hurried footsteps; it was the private returning with Captain Vergara and others of the staff. He heard their exclamations of astonishment, and their hurried debate on what should be done. Then came a sharp order from the captain.

"March your men back to the compound, Corporal."

And back to their dreary ten acres of barbed-wire enclosure went the fourth chain-gang; from it they could see corpulent old General Aranguren hastening across from his house to the scene of the discovery, while from all over the island the other gangs were marched hurriedly back to the compound, to be locked safely away behind the barbed-wire. Dawkins' discovery had at least gained for every convict on the island a cessation of labor two hours before time.

CHAPTER IV

IN THE prisoners' compound the spectacle was little different from what was usual. Most of the prisoners lay huddled like exhausted animals, many of them in little hollows which they had scraped in the phosphate, and which, if needs were, they would defend against their fellows with teeth and claws like animals. A few of the less apathetic sat in a chattering group discussing the wonderful find of the afternoon.

One man alone was on his feet, tramping up and down against the bars of his cage, and that man was Henry Dawkins. His mind was in a turmoil quite unusual, his fists were clenched, and even his heart was beating with a distressing violence. Somehow the recent event had roused him to a wild panicky desire for freedom, in contrast to his more usual dull, aching hatred of Birds Island, of the forced labor and of his jailers. He knew —he *knew*—that Corporal Barroso had a pocket-

ful of jewels worth a king's ransom, but his dull
mind could not work out a scheme by which he
could make use of his knowledge. He might tell
some one higher in authority—and that would be
none to easy to contrive—but it would only result
in Barroso's punishment and the confiscation of
the jewels. They would not set free in exchange
the Hawk's lieutenant-general, condemned to
forced labor for life on Birds Island. Barroso
would see to that. Dawkins continued to rage im-
potently up and down the edge of the tangled
barbed-wire which hemmed him in, up and down,
up and down, until night fell gloomy over the
purple sea and over the misery of the island.

Dawkins never knew how the next development
came about. He never really had the chance of
finding out, but the explanation was quite simple.
Captain Vergara, the company officer who had
come to inspect the treasure on its first discovery,
was a man of bold ambition and vast greed. He
had seen two hundredweights of gold and half a
ton of silver borne off at General Aranguren's
orders up to the adobe house which represented
the seat of government. The general, poor spiritless fool, had no other thought than to turn over

this heaped-up pirate treasure to his government—
to President Eguia, in other words. Captain Vergara could not conceive of such folly. If the captain had had charge of such a mass of treasure
Eguia would never see a ha'p'orth of it; the captain
would not stay an hour on the island longer than
was necessary to transfer the gold to the motor-
boat which rocked beside the jetty. It was a prize
worth fighting for, Vergara had decided, and before night fell he was already cautiously sounding
his company to discover whether they thought so,
too.

Not much time was wasted in discussion. Every
minute was of value if the blow was to be struck
before betrayal was possible. Vergara's sergeants,
dazzled at the prospect of a thousand dollars
apiece (and, possibly, each with an eye to the possibility of repeating later the same scheme on his
own behalf after the governor was out of the
way), pledged themselves enthusiastically to an
attack on the other company of the garrison. They
could answer for their men, they said. Some of
the rank and file would fight at any call whatso-
ever; some would obey their sergeants automatically; one and all would fight on a promise of gold

and drink and women. Vergara issued his orders briefly to his sergeants, and dismissed them to make all ready; he had not troubled to take his subaltern officers into his confidence, for they would demand so large a share of the plunder as to make their deaths eminently desirable. So as night fell Captain Vergara's company assembled here and there over Birds Island, in driblets and platoons; for fortune was on Vergara's side in that it was his company's turn to supply the guards and duty men for the day.

The moon rose, serene, untroubled and three-quarters full. It looked down upon the prisoners' compound—a big square enclosed by a broad belt of barbed wire. At one corner the broad belt was wanting, being replaced by two successive gates of wood hung thickly with barbed wire, with a clear space between in which, in the mornings, the gangs were one by one chained ready for the day's work. Outside the outer gate was an adobe tower which served as a guard-house, and on whose flat top were mounted the two machine-guns which could sweep the compound clear in case of mutiny. Here stayed the prison guard which was not on sentry duty, each side of the wire compound had three sentries; and there were two posted outside the gates. President Eguia, when he had organized the Birds Island Convict Colony (as it was euphemistically called officially), had borne in mind that sentries and barbed wire will hold prisoners far more effectively than stone walls or iron bars—besides being infinitely cheaper. The expense to which Eguia was put per head of prisoners (one can be sure he worked it out carefully enough) amounted to a few hundred yards of barbed wire and two blankets, for the men had nothing else, literally nothing — no roof, no clothes, no furniture, but lived like beasts in the open enclosure.

Dawkins, huddled sleepless in his blanket on the edge of the compound, gazed out through the strange shadows cast by the moon. He looked to see the silhouettes of the sentries on the other side of the belt of wire. He could see nothing. He looked for the sentries on the gate. Again he could see nothing. He sat up and rubbed his eyes, disbelieving his senses. He looked carefully again, but he could see no sign of the guard. Then he saw a long file of soldiers, rifle in hand, moving silently out from beyond the guard-house round the enclosure. The moonlight was strangely deceptive, but he made an effort to count them. There were at least fifty men in the party, enough to account for every private, sergeant and bugler in the prison guard. They moved silently past the compound and on up the slight slope to where shone the lighted windows of the governor's house. Dawkins crouched down close to the ground as they went by. His soldier's instinct told him that it might be as well if he was thought to be asleep, although so far he could not for the life of him guess what was going on.

It was unfortunate for Captain Vergara's plans that General Aranguren's aide-de-camp should have been taking the night air outside the general's house. Captain Vergara had visualized a sudden bloodless capture of the treasure, the overawing of the surprised remainder of the garrison, and a rapid departure next day. But the meddlesome aide spoiled all this. He observed the advance of the long line of men through the shadows. He challenged, received no reply, challenged again, and was fired at (and, of course, missed) by a hot-headed private in the ranks. The aide just had time to rush into the house and slam the door as the attacking party rose of one accord and charged forward.

General Aranguren, his aides-de-camp and his servants did their duty and died for it. As the stormers burst in through the windows and the doors, they caught up whatever weapons came to hand and fought for five furious minutes before the last of them fell and the house with its treasure and its women was delivered over to the mercy of Captain Vergara and his followers.

The sudden explosion of rifle and revolver fire reached the ears both of those in the prison camp and of those in the military hutments on the other side. The other company of infantry came crowding out at the noise, and once more excess of zeal on the part of Vergara's men precipitated events. For the line of pickets which Vergara had thrown out toward the hutments opened fire on the swarming mass of men, and these, not unnaturally aggrieved, rushed back for their weapons and opened a retaliatory fire. No sooner had Captain Vergara obtained satisfactory possession of General Aranguren's house and treasure than he found himself with another battle on his hands. Tempers were short on Birds Island, and the soldiers were inflamed by the knowledge of the discovery of the treasure. Before very long the whole of the other company of infantry had automatically extended itself in a long firing-line centering upon the hutments, blazing away in the deceptive moonlight at the similar firing-line formed by such of Vergara's men as Vergara, mad with rage, could force away from the pillaging of the governor's house.

The prisoners in the compound awoke one and all when the firing began. They heard the storming of the house, and they heard the splutter of fire of the new battle swell rapidly into a wild volume of sound. They crowded up to the wire to see what was going on, but in that half-light they could only make out the red flashes of some of the rifles without distinguishing any of the features of the battle. Some stray bullets came crackling overhead; one came lower, smashed the elbow of one of the onlookers, and left him yelling with pain on the ground while the others hurriedly scattered.

Henry Dawkins stood by the barbed-wire gate and peered forth. He was looking away from the battle; eighteen months of guerrilla warfare against Spanish-American troops enabled him to guess automatically the cause and course and probable result of the skirmish. He was most interested in discovering whether the machine-gun tower was manned or not, and both deduction (from his estimate of the number of men he had seen pass) and observation on the spot told him it was not. Nor was it—that was another of the many blunders Captain Vergara had committed in his clumsy attempt on the treasure. As soon as Dawkins was sure of this, he turned back toward the others with an instinctive plan fermenting in his mind. He caught up an armful of the blankets that littered the ground, he tugged at the sleeves of the men within reach, he shouted and he called. At first only some half-dozen followed his lead; the rest were too apathetic, too panic-stricken, or too dull of mind—besides, the grim menace of the machine-gun tower, during months of imprisonment, had left its trace on the reactions of most of them.

But the efforts of half a dozen were sufficient. Blankets were flung round strands of the wire gate, and the ends were pulled until the wire broke. Dawkins and a couple of others, more clear-headed, knotted together four or five blankets into a rope long enough to pass over the whole gate. The others, desisting from their more ineffective efforts, tailed on as well, and amid a howl of triumph the whole gate was dragged down and out of the way—a success gained at the cost of a good many frightful lacerations from the wire, but the haggled cuts passed unnoticed in the excitement of the moment. By this time the attention of the whole prison camp was drawn to the gates, and all the two hundred convicts swarmed forward to the second gate.

This latter held out a little longer, thanks to the blundering manner in which two hundred excited men hampered one another's efforts, but it yielded in the end, and all the prisoners came rushing out, tearing themselves fearfully on stray strands of barbed wire, trampling underfoot those who fell, and proclaiming, by their wild yells, to the opposed companies of infantry that two hundred maddened criminals were let loose on their flank. Some of the startled soldiers fired wildly into the dark mass of men as it came surging out in the moonlight, but the surprise was too great to be withstood. Both the long thin firing lines crumpled up and drifted away across the island, still firing at each other, at the escaped prisoners, and of course, in their panic, at themselves, while the prisoners, masterless and leaderless, broke up into a swarm of raging madmen scattering hither and thither, some making blindly for the sea, some racing for the stores of food and drink in the sheds behind the soldiers' huts, while a few blundered upon the adobe walled compound of the female prisoners—and stayed there. The whole island was soon dotted with men, armed and unarmed, in ones and twos, firing wildly at whomever came near, grappling in the half-light and fighting to the death with whomever they met, killing, fleeing, plundering, to the accompaniment of the flame and crackle of the rifle-fire and the eternal thunder of the surf.

CHAPTER V

DAWKINS was perhaps the only one of the prisoners who made any attempt at clear thinking in that mad rush from the gates. There were two things he wanted. One was to get away from the island, and the other was to find Corporal Barroso and to take from him the pocketful of jewels which Dawkins was certain he had. Dawkins may have been far from quick-witted, but even as he ran he made a whole series of mental deductions. He realized that a man with a fortune in jewels in his pocket would not willingly involve himself in the wild battle which was being fought; he guessed that he would try to get away from the island as speedily as he could, and he came to the conclusion that if Barroso were on the island he would be near the jetty, where the motor-boat was which alone could take him, or any one else on Birds Island, out of the reach of President Eguia. Dawkins swung sharply aside, and ran, heavily but purposefully and speedily, down

50

to the jetty along the faint trail which had been worn by the myriad feet of the working parties.

Down the path went Dawkins, single-minded and grim. He halted in the shadow of the big pile of phosphate sacks at the shore end of the jetty and peered out. For the moment he could see no sign of Barroso. The dingey was not in its usual place at the pier-side; instead he could see it swinging close to where the big motor-launch was moored, a quarter of a mile from shore. He strained his ears and his eyes, trying to sift out from the bedlam of noises behind him any slight noise from the boat. He thought he heard such a noise; he thought he saw a man's head over the gunwale of the launch. Dawkins put aside all thought of the sharks which sometimes came nosing within the coral, and slipped silently into the sea, swimming powerfully toward the launch.

Corporal Barroso was experiencing a burst of panic fear. On his person he bore wealth beyond his wildest dreams. Here he was, established in a motor-boat which would take him two hundred miles away, beyond reach of Eguia or Aranguren or Vergara. His limited imagination could picture himself established in a white palace on the hills overlooking Valparaiso, with men servants and maid servants, living that life of luxurious ease for which his soul hungered. It was within his reach —save that he did not know how to start the engine of the motor-boat. The dingey seemed to his mind too small to encounter the big Pacific swell. Somewhere within him Barroso's little soul tried to assure him that in this case his best policy would be to go back and plunge into the strife on the island, and await some other chance of escape, seeing that no one knew of his possession of the jewels, but Barroso's shrinking body could not face the prospect. He blundered on round the motor-launch in the darkness, racking his numb brain to recall the various successive operations of starting the engine—operations he had only casually observed.

And as he fumbled with chattering teeth, something made him look up. Two hands were clutching the side of the boat, and above and between them appeared a big head, shrouded in a tangle of hair. The head was followed by two broad shoulders, and a knee appeared beside the hands, before Barroso recovered sufficiently to reach for his rifle. Even as his fingers touched it, Dawkins' big bulk heaved itself over the gunwale and fell upon him with crushing force.

The two men writhed and pitched about in the well of the launch. Dawkins' big calloused hands reached Barroso's throat. They were vast hands, powerful hands, and the palms were half an inch thick with horn. Barroso's struggles suddenly became more frantic and as suddenly ceased. Dawkins heaved himself up to his knees, but Barroso lay limp, his cat's-whisker mustache perky in the moonlight, curiously belying the pathetic helplessness of his dead body.

But Dawkins was not the man to moralize or to waste time. He ran rapid fingers through the pockets of Barroso's drab gray uniform, turning the body backward and forward as though it were a doll. It was not long before he found what he sought—a cloth bag which gave forth a curious, distinctive, stony chink when shaken. Nowhere in Dawkins' ragged shirt or shorts was there any pocket, but with cool rapidity he tied the bag into the tail of his shirt, stuffed it back into his shorts, and made a last examination of Barroso's pockets for anything that might be useful. A few coins he stuffed into his cheek—the prisoners on Birds

Island soon learned that was the safest place of all for money—but nothing else took his fancy. Then with the same calm haste he picked up the body and dropped it overboard, instinctively doing all he could to conceal evidence of his crime. Barroso sank with hardly a ripple, down through the dark sea where the shark and octopus awaited him. That was all the good his jewels had done him.

Dawkins continued his plan of campaign, more than half instinctively, with the experience gained by eighteen months of guerrilla warfare. A few seconds told him that he, no more than Barroso, knew not how to start the engine of the motor-launch. A few minutes' experiment in daylight would show him, very probably, but Dawkins decided resolutely not to wait the five hours till dawn. It was the dingey or nothing, then, and Dawkins decided that the dingey, frail though it was, would serve his purpose, for the weather was calm, and seemed likely to remain so. He saw that oars lay in the dingey, but a quick examination showed him that neither in the launch nor in the dingey was there food or water; and these he must have before he steered out into the Pacific. Again his fierce soldier's instinct asserted itself. He could not take the chance of drawing attention to himself and to his boat by rowing back to the jetty without being able to start away again at once. He lowered himself into the sea, reached the shore and walked hurriedly along to the barracks.

Here stood in a line the soldiers' huts, the store-houses, the distilling plant and the cook-houses; and here blazed a big fire. Scattered about were some hundred of the escaped prisoners, some of them lying dead or drunk already, most of them grouped in threes and fours about the brandy casks which had been dragged from the store-house. They yelled and they sang and they tried to dance; beside the fire lay a huddled group which included half a dozen half-naked women from the women's compound, clasped and tangled in hide-ous attitudes. Mingled with the prisoners were even some few soldiers in their drab uniforms, swilling brandy out of mugs.

Dawkins paid no attention to any of them, not even to the shouts of one or two who recognized him. Already he could foresee what would happen in the morning, when the soldiers would sink their differences and would sweep down upon the buildings, slaughtering every soul they found. Dawkins did not know, nor did he care, what would happen next; that was enough for him. He found a big iron cooking-vessel with a lid, and filled it with water at the still. He filled a panier with bread, and, loaded in a fashion which brought forth the sweat in streams down his chilled body, he staggered back to the jetty.

Once more he took to the water, bringing back the dingey to where his stores awaited him, and then, setting his course by the stars, he rowed westward away from the island, away from the mainland. Even now there were occasional flashes and reports from the island, where the skirmish still bickered on.

Barroso lay at the bottom of the lagoon with his neck wrung. General Aranguren lay with his household, with twenty bullets through him. Captain Vergara lay on the crest of Birds Island with a bullet through his heart. A score of other corpses lay hither and thither on the island, and six score more would be added to their number when daylight came. The pirates who, a hundred and fifty years ago, had buried their plunder on Birds Island, had had no good of it—for was not the treasure left all that time untouched? And they in their turn had plundered and looted the towns of the mainland to obtain it, while before that Spanish taskmasters had burned Incas to death and had caused Indian and negro slaves to die under the lash for the precious gain. And now, after all that, the diamonds and the pearls and the rubies were crudely bound into the ragged shirt-tail of the man who was rowing a frail dingey out westerly over the Pacific rollers under the paling stars. He was rowing, rowing, rowing, tirelessly, automatically, with the strength and the endurance fostered by months of forced labor. Rowing, rowing, rowing, in his tossing cockle-shell. When dawn came Birds Island was only a speck on the horizon.

CHAPTER VI

AWKINS had taken a monstrous risk when he had launched himself in his little boat out on to the Pacific, but, as he had decided in his balanced fashion, it was not so great a risk as it would have been to remain on the island. And, moreover, he knew that fifty miles to the west of Birds Island lay the main route of the coastwise traffic; many times from the crest of Birds Island had he seen on the horizon the faint smudge of a steamer's smoke. Yet it can hardly be denied that he was extremely fortunate to be picked up on his third morning by the steel four-masted bark *Hammerfest,* Norwegian owned, in ballast from San Francisco to Punta Arenas.

There was not an Englishman on board the *Hammerfest* (Englishmen are scarce on Scandinavian sailing ships), but the Swedish captain and the grave mystic Norwegians and Finns received him with kindness. They even asked fewer questions than their scant broken English would have

58

permitted. Dawkins explained with due reticence
that he was an escaped convict from the penal settlement on Birds Island, and they nodded sympathetically. Grim tales were already being told
along the Rainless Coast about the horrors perpe-
trated on Birds Island, although of course the
Hammerfest knew nothing of the late mutiny, and
one glimpse of Dawkins' back, all seamed and
corrugated with scars, made the crew his fast
friends. Any lingering fear that Dawkins might
have had that he would be handed back to the justice of the Rainless Republic was dispelled by the
kindness of his reception. The captain even went
so far as to offer Dawkins a passage in the *Hammerfest* to London River, after loading with wheat
at Punta Arenas, and the offer was gladly accepted, especially as the offer included a quiet
landing at London Docks without the formalities
of a police inquiry. But even with all this kindness
heaped upon him, with a berth with the boatswain
and sailmaker and a place at the officers' table
given him, Dawkins did not see fit to inform any
one that, tied in the tail of his shirt, he had a parcel
of jewels worth ten times as much as the *Hammerfest* and her cargo put together. Captain Andersen

found him clothes from the ship's stores, and when Dawkins hinted that he had wealthy friends in London who would make due repayment Andersen put the matter gravely to one side. The clothes were poor and the accommodation bad and the food scanty, as was only to be expected in a Norwegian wind-jammer, but somehow the unquestioning kindness touched Dawkins perceptibly; he could hardly remember receiving any other kindness during thirty-five years of a hard life.

And so the *Hammerfest* ran on southward into the tall seas and eternal westerly winds, turned eastward through the towering cliffs of the Straits of Magellan, and cast anchor in Punta Arenas. Here, while the ballast was discharged and the cargo shipped, Dawkins remained discreetly out of the way of casual observation—with Captain Andersen's voiceless approval. For at Punta Arenas the news of the fearful outbreak at Birds Island, which cost the lives of a hundred soldiers and a hundred and fifty convicts, was already to hand— such news as leaked out despite President Eguia's careful censorship. Dawkins observed that Captain Andersen was looking at him sometimes with a puzzled expression, but he was asked no further questions. Captain Andersen, at the back of his slow Swedish mind, could draw a sufficiently vivid mental picture of the blood and slaughter of the mutiny, and he did not care very much how much blood was on Dawkins' hands; he fancied there was a great deal more than there actually was.

For Dawkins was a somber and an impressive figure, with his huge shoulders and hands, and his mass of tawny hair and beard, and the fierce scowl on his narrow brow above his narrowed blue eyes. He said nothing for days together, while the *Hammerfest* came crashing home across the Atlantic, and it was not his total lack of Norwegian nor the other's partial lack of English which held him silent. He had lost the habit of speech in the prison compound on Birds Island—and besides, his brain was busy with a manifold complexity of thoughts. He would stand by the wheel speechless for hours, with his glance shifting slowly and casually from the full-drawing canvas to the sea, pondering over what possibly lay before him in the future.

Dawkins had the mind of a man of action, not that of a dreamer. Confronted with a sudden emergency and a desperate need to act immediately he would react brilliantly and instinctively, as he had done on Birds Island and a hundred times before that, but plotting and planning were not so much in his line. He had been outplotted before, by a thieving pawnbroker's assistant in England, just after the war, which was why he had left England in a hurry, and ultimately why he had joined the Hawk's insurgent army and been sent to Birds Island. Not that he was not guilty; he had been guilty all right, but he had been lacking in the finesse to avoid discovery. It was one more example of the curious way in which the world is constructed, that a man of Dawkins' thews and sinews and heavy mentality should have been, first, a pawnbroker's assistant, and, second, that he should have been subjected to the temptation to which he fell. But Dawkins' family was, as has already been mentioned, a younger line of the great pawnbroking family of Dawkins, so that it is not altogether surprising.

So that while the gray skies of the Horn were being succeeded by the blue skies of the Tropics, and then by the clear freshness of the Trades, Henry Dawkins was trying to plan his future. A man with something over a hundred thousand pounds in precious stones tied in his shirt-tail (for he continued to use that hiding-place, as the most convenient) has need to consider his next step warily.

Money, just as money, had indeed a certain definite appeal for him. He felt a thrill of pleasure at the anticipation of being rich. But he had small notion of what he wanted his riches to give him. Women and wine of course bulked large in the faint picture. Lust he knew; it had taken him by the throat and rendered him captive many times before this, when he had been a younger man and on leave from active service in France. He supposed, philosophically, that it would do the same again as soon as he set foot on shore. And he felt a glow of warm anticipation such as he could remember of old. Drink? The freedom of being able to drink, yes, but Dawkins did not look forward to lots of drink. A year of total abstention on Birds Island had blunted that desire, just as it had sharpened the other one. All the sins of Sodom and Gomorrah had festered and smoldered in the prison compound, though; Dawkins' nose wrinkled with distaste at the memory of things seen.

His yearning for vague women and vaguer drinks was dulled by the need he was impressing upon himself for caution at the start. A debauch descried faintly through the turns and twists of a preliminary policy holds small appeal, and Dawkins was rigidly holding himself to the resolution that he must not relax until the plunder in his shirt-tail was properly disposed of—he could foresee how necessary it would be to be cautious, even though only the faint outline of a plan was in his mind.

And then, above and beyond all these other considerations, there was running continually through Dawkins' mind the memory of a promise made to the Hawk—a promise made to a dying man. "Sixty-one Field Hill, Norwood," said Dawkins to himself, over and over again. It was an address he had carried in his mind during a whole year in the prison camp on Birds Island; it was the address of the Hawk's stepmother in England, where the Hawk had left his daughter on setting out on his last unlucky journey to the Rainless Coast. Dawkins had promised, if ever he found his way home, to seek out this Miss Royle and tell her that her father was dead, and, if possible, to see that she wanted for nothing. The memory of this promise was small comfort to Dawkins. Although he had made it when he expected nothing more than death by torture at Eguia's hands, and was now prepared to fulfill it as a man of wealth, the mission did not attract him at all. He had loved the Hawk even while he feared him, and the thought of telling his daughter (whom he pictured in his mind as an exceedingly able woman, sensitive and mercurial like the Hawk himself) of his death raised grim apprehension in his mind.

So that Dawkins had ample food for thought as he paced moodily about the deck of the *Hammerfest*. Officers and men thought him fey, and left him severely alone—for which he was grateful. He had offered, in his sullen awkward fashion, to help in the work of the ship, but, short-handed though the *Hammerfest* was, in common with all Scandinavian ships, his proffered unskilled labor was declined. The favorable weather which accompanied the *Hammerfest* all the way from the Virgins to Ushant even excited the superstitious fears of the Finns and Norwegians; they thought that somehow this burly bearded stranger was responsible for the snorting southwesterly gales which drove them homeward on what was nearly a record passage, and they gave him a wide berth in consequence. Dawkins grew gloomier and more self-contained every day of the trip, and felt no thrill of elation even when they picked up English lights at nightfall, nor when dawn revealed the English coast on the port beam.

Uneventfully they picked up their pilot and their tug, and at evening one autumn day they came stealing into London Docks. Dawkins and the ship's officers bade each other unemotional good-bys, and directly afterward, baggageless and free, Dawkins made an unobtrusive landing.

CHAPTER VII

MR. SIMPSON was just beginning to consider closing down his shop. His assistants had had their eyes on the clock for the last hour, and were now fidgeting restlessly as a hint to Mr. Simpson to give the word. A strange little man was Mr. Simpson, with his bald head and his dead-fish eyes, but he was a very successful man. It is the good fortune of few to combine successfully the professions of pawnbroking and receiving stolen goods, but Mr. Simpson had carried on undetected for years, even at the cost of a rumored bad name in confidential pawnbroking circles. His little East End shop served admirably as a screen for his other activities from the eyes of the police.

Just as Mr. Simpson was about to give the word to close the shop the door opened and some one entered with a heavy tread. The assistants looked at him with annoyance, Mr. Simpson with interest. He was very tall and very powerfully built, dressed in a badly fitting suit of clothes which obviously came from a merchant ship's slop-chest, and his features were blurred by a big tawny beard and a shock of tawny hair. Mr. Simpson was chiefly conscious of the gaze of a pair of fierce, puzzled, blue eyes beneath a scowling desperate brow. The newcomer slipped his hand in his pocket and looked round hesitatingly. He made as though to speak to an assistant, hesitated, withdrew his hand and put it back again. The facial expression, the gestures, the sequence of behavior all told Mr. Simpson the reason of his entrance; Mr. Simpson did not, of course, know that Dawkins of dire necessity was acting superbly a part which he had been rehearsing all the way from Punta Arenas.

"Do you want to speak to me, mister?" asked Mr. Simpson, and Dawkins nodded.

"Then just come in here a moment. Brown, you see to shutting up."

And Mr. Simpson ushered Dawkins into his little private office, thanking his stars that this blundering sailor had come into the shop and had not entered one of the little confessional boxes round the corner where perhaps an assistant would have attended to him. Mr. Simpson switched on an additional light over the green baize table and waited, running his eyes keenly over his visitor. Those clothes, those big horny hands, that lumbering gait, indicated the sailor to Mr. Simpson as plainly as words could have done; the mistake was at least pardonable, but Mr. Simpson could not at present guess with any certainty at the nationality of his visitor.

"Well?" asked Mr. Simpson.

For answer Dawkins drew from his pocket a little cloth bag, hardly bigger than a glove finger, and emptied it upon the green baize table. Six perfect large pearls rolled upon the cloth, all of them rose pink, four of them round and two of them drop shape—a magnificent pair.

"Ah," said Mr. Simpson. "Um."

He stretched out a finger and rolled them over. He held them to the light. He screwed a lens into his eye and gazed at them through that. He weighed them in his palm, and then (although so delicate was his touch that such an operation was almost unnecessary) he weighed them on his jeweler's scales.

"What d'you want to do with these? Pawn them?" he asked.

"Sell 'em," was the laconic rejoinder.

"Um," said Mr. Simpson again. Then, suddenly, "What ship are you off?"

"*Hammerfest,*" answered Mr. Dawkins throatily, "from 'Frisco."

"Ah," said Mr. Simpson, thinking rapidly. He knew of the extensive trade in stolen pearls carried on in San Francisco, and he saw nothing surprising in a sailor from thence having pearls in his possession. But still he could not guess at Dawkins' nationality.

"Why did you come here?" asked Mr. Simpson, firing his question suddenly, hoping to take Dawkins off his guard.

"Mr. Jones told me."

"Where did you see him?"

" 'Frisco."

"Um," said Mr. Simpson again.

He knew no Mr. Jones, and especially no Mr. Jones of 'Frisco, but that did not mean the stranger was lying. For the man who told him might (and probably did) have very good reason for using a false name. But this big stupid Swede (Mr. Simp-

son had almost made up his mind that Dawkins
was a Swede) was not laying any trap; Mr. Simpson was sure of it.

"These aren't any use to me," said Mr. Simpson.
"They're too well known."

"Not well known. New 'uns."

That was perfectly true, as Mr. Simpson realized. No pearls of this class had been lately stolen,
as far as Mr. Simpson's knowledge—which was
fairly extensive, he flattered himself—went.

"What's your name, anyway?" asked Mr. Simpson, changing the subject in an abrupt fashion,
which he had frequently found useful.

"Hansen," replied Dawkins stolidly. "Ole Hansen."

"Well, all I can say, Mr. Hansen, is—take 'em
away. They're no use to me. Take 'em away."

Unmoved and immobile of feature, Dawkins began slowly to replace the pearls in the little bag.

"Oh, blast it all," said the exasperated Mr.
Simpson. "Here, let's have another look at 'em."

He stared at them again, lingeringly, through
his lens at each in turn.

"Give you a fiver for 'em," he said at length
grudgingly.

"Twenty-five," said Dawkins heavily.

"Not worth it. Five's as far as I can go. Six perhaps."

"Twenty-five," said Dawkins again.

Mr. Simpson's fingers itched and twittered. Twenty-five pounds was exactly the top limit of what he was prepared to pay for these pearls worth a hundred and fifty, but it cut him to the quick to have to hand over all that money to a lumbering Swede who would probably squander every penny that same night. Brown, his trusted henchman, was in the outer office, and the other clerks had gone. But Mr. Simpson, although he had an automatic pistol under his left armpit, could not contemplate violence with fifteen stone of berserk strength within two yards of him. Perhaps cunning could replace violence.

" 'ere, 'ave a drink," said Mr. Simpson, opening a wall cupboard and revealing a whisky bottle with glasses and siphons all tantalizingly displayed.

But Dawkins' wooden expression did not change.

"No," he said rudely enough. "Do you want these?"

He pointed at the pearls with a blunt horny finger, and he made a significant gesture with the little bag in his other hand.

"Look 'ere, I'll give you ten for 'em, and take a chance," said Mr. Simpson.

"Twenty-five," said Dawkins.

Mr. Simpson rebelled against this inflexible demand. He slapped the table pettishly; he gesticulated vehemently; he argued and he pleaded. But simultaneously his offers rose, a pound or so at a time. He shed a tear or two when they reached eighteen.

"Twenty-five," said Dawkins, inexorable as fate.

Mr. Simpson took a drink, but again his offer of one was refused monosyllabically.

"Well, twenty, then," said Mr. Simpson desperately.

"Twenty-five," said Dawkins, and Simpson realized at last that he really meant it. Even the cunning Mr. Simpson had not guessed that Dawkins would have been seriously embarrassed if Mr. Simpson had been sincere when he told Dawkins to take the pearls away.

Mr. Simpson produced the money. He made a moment's play with five-pound notes, but a passionate gesture from Dawkins made him put them away again. The money was handed over in one-pound notes, which Dawkins stuffed into his breast pocket. And then Dawkins withdrew by a series of well-planned movements—so well planned that their elaboration of caution almost passed unnoticed. He opened the door behind him with his back to it and his face to Mr. Simpson, passed through backward with inconspicuous haste, wheeled to meet the faithful Brown, and strode through to the outside door, which Brown, a little unprepared, unlocked for him. In the next instant Dawkins was through into the outer darkness, before Mr. Simpson in the inner chamber had finished locking his safe. It was two seconds after Dawkins had disappeared before Mr. Simpson leaped into the outer shop.

" 'ave you let 'im go, you something fool?" demanded Simpson. "Foller 'im then, quick. Find out 'oo 'e is and where 'e's staying. Quick, you pie-can."

But two seconds is all a man needs to evade pursuit when he knows he is going to be pursued. The faithful Brown could gain no sight anywhere of a tall bearded Swede. Later, a couple of days'

detective work on the part of Mr. Simpson discovered that a ship *Hammerfest* had undoubtedly
come in that day from 'Frisco, and that she undoubtedly had on board a seaman called Hansen.

But when Mr. Simpson at last tracked down this
Hansen he found he resembled the man with the
pearls in no way whatever—a discovery which irri-
tated and worried Mr. Simpson profoundly, so
that he parted with the six pearls to an Amsterdam
dealer with such precipitation as to cost him a good
deal of money. And, after all, there was no danger
to any one of established position about selling
those pearls. Dawkins had only chosen that method to obtain a quick sale and no questions asked.

That was the last night that the tawny beard and
the mop of hair were to be seen, for Mr. Dawkins,
safely back in his sailor's lodging-house, spent a
grisly half-hour with scissors and razor removing
them. He had taken these simple precautions because he had over a hundred thousand pounds'
worth of precious stones on his person, and he
wanted neither to risk losing them nor to have any
ghosts appearing from the past when he reached
that moneyed future which lay within his grasp.

CHAPTER VIII

MR. DAWKINS spent a wakeful night, and small blame to him, either. He turned backward and forward in his bed in the little room beside the Mile End Road; he got up and walked about the room; he sat uncomfortably on the single wooden chair, listening to the occasional traffic outside. It was not that he was frightened or worried; he told himself that he was not even excited, although that is to be doubted. He was unsettled and on the brink of great events, and in the faint light which came in through the windows (in that economical lodging-house lights were turned off at midnight) he was conjuring up faint visions of the future.

But they were exasperatingly faint, for Dawkins simply did not know what he wanted to happen. He could not picture himself with a hundred thousand pounds in the bank and nothing to do all day. His method of converting jewels into cash had been sufficiently worked out, to his mind, and

the execution of it lay immediately before him.
But after that, what? Mr. Dawkins did not know.
Imprisonment, as penologists discover and announce daily, unfits one for liberty. Mr. Dawkins
swore softly to himself and climbed back into bed
again, to lie awake until the first daylight began to
leak in through the window and the early factory
whistles made themselves heard. The life of the
lodging-house began to stir again, at last, and Mr.
Dawkins sighed with relief and started to put on
his trousers. A night he would long remember was
finished, and a day, every detail of which he had
thought out beforehand, was about to begin.

Mr. Dawkins paid his little bill, ignoring the
landlady's start of surprise at sight of his haggled
hair and missing beard, and came out into the chill
morning. A bus, crammed with early workers,
took him through the City to the Strand, where he
breakfasted at leisure and with some comfort.
Next he called at a barber's, and had himself
smartened up. When the barber had finished with
him he looked at himself long in the glass. What
he saw was strange and unreal to him; he saw a
man in the late thirties, his face bronzed and
wrinkled, with hard lines round the fierce blue

eyes. The mouth, tight shut, would have told a disinterested observer of profound suffering and of grim determination. The upper lip was adorned with a neatly clipped mustache of a golden tawny, and the hair was parted at the side and brushed smoothly away from the knotted forehead. What surprised Dawkins most was the fact that the barber's attentions had made him look quite like a gentleman, as he put it to himself—a sunburned face and a tall figure and a clipped mustache is the normal English visualization of a gentleman; although he realized how incongruous his well-groomed head looked compared with his slop clothes.

From the barber's Mr. Dawkins proceeded to a printer's, where he ordered some plain visiting cards—"Mr. Henry Dawkins"—to be prepared at once, and from the printer's Mr. Dawkins took his way to a vast and well-advertised gentleman's outfitters, where commissionnaires and shop-walkers received him dubiously. But Mr. Dawkins ignored their doubts, and proceeded to select a complete new set of clothes. In the tailoring department the fitter ran an appreciative eye over Mr. Dawkins' tall stout figure, and justified the proud boast of

his firm's advertisements by finding at once a suit
which fitted him miraculously, forty-two-inch chest
and all. He was so pleased that he did not notice
the anxious way in which Mr. Dawkins kept watch
on his coat while it was off—there was a big parcel
of precious stones in one pocket thereof. Mr.
Dawkins hesitated a moment over blue and brown
and gray, and finally chose navy blue as neatest
and least conspicuous. They showed him pretty
colored shirts and collars of blue and brown, but
Mr. Dawkins chose white for the same reason, and
a black tie, and medium weight underwear, and
neat black shoes and socks, and a gray soft hat and
light overcoat. Gloves and walking stick completed his purchases, and he suffered the assistants
to shut him up in a mirror-lined dressing-room to
change.

And when the change was completed, and Mr.
Dawkins had his twenty pounds' worth of clothing
on his back, he looked in the mirror with more
astonishment than ever. The well-fitting clothes,
despite their brand-newness, set off his burly figure
to perfection, and the clipped mustache and neat
head no longer seemed incongruous. Mr. Dawkins, hat, stick and gloves in hand, and light over-

coat open down the front, with his air of assurance, heightened by his powerful frame, looked every inch a man of wealth and position—a fact curiously reflected in the changed behavior of shop assistants and commissionnaires.

Leaving his other clothes in a parcel to be called for, Mr. Dawkins strolled back to the printer's and collected his visiting cards, and two doors away he bought a card-case. Then he took his way leisurely toward where City and West End meet, and turned northward. A reference to a telephone directory reassured him that the man he was seeking was still in business at his old address; even the most carefully made plans ignore some possibilities of error, and Mr. Dawkins realized that he had made all these preparations for the impressing of Mr. Carver's office boy without finding out first whether or not Mr. Carver still lived. It might have been serious, but as it happened it was all right.

Mr. Dawkins walked calmly into Mr. Carver's office. He was about to put his fortune to the test, and he was conscious of a rise in blood-pressure and a quickened pulse, but he held himself in with an iron hand and betrayed no trace of emotion as he asked for "Mr. Carver?" when the office boy asked his business. He handed over a card nonchalantly, sat down in the proffered chair, and gazed calmly about him.

Dawkins was aware of his good fortune in having once been a pawnbroker; it was in consequence of this experience that he knew about the seamier side of the jeweler's trade; he knew who had good reputations and who had bad, and who might have a bad reputation if more were known about them. Mr. Adam Carver, diamond merchant, belonged to this last category.

"Mr. Carver says will you come up, sir?" said the office boy. Mr. Dawkins' plain visiting card had of course given no hint of his business, and his name conveyed little. What had turned the scale had been Mr. Dawkins' twenty pounds' worth of clothes and the office boy's report upon them. Mr. Dawkins had not the look of a tiresome commercial traveler.

"Good morning, Mr.—er Dawkins," said Mr. Carver, with a last glance at the card.

"Good morning," said Mr. Dawkins, sitting in the armchair on the other side of the desk.

The two looked at each other curiously, although Carver had the advantage because, of course, Dawkins had the light on his face.

"And what can I do for you?" asked Mr. Carver.

For answer Mr. Dawkins produced from his vest pocket a wisp of tissue-paper and handed it over; when Mr. Carver opened it he revealed a large, white, brilliant-cut diamond. Carver went through a series of actions curiously reminiscent of Mr. Simpson's the night before. He peered at the diamond, hefted it, handled it and put it down again.

"Brazilian," he said. "Good water. Old-fashioned cut. What about it?"

"I've got a lot to sell," said Mr. Dawkins.

Mr. Carver's eyebrows went up a shade.

"A lot?"

"A good many thousand pounds' worth. A hundred and fifty, perhaps. Perhaps more."

Mr. Carver's eyebrows rose higher still, until there seemed to be a danger of their colliding with the hair on the top of his head—and there was not much room between them at the best of times.

"And do you want me to buy 'em?"

"I should like you to sell 'em for me."

Mr. Carver was dazzlingly interested but exceedingly cautious.

"It doesn't sound the sort of thing I could touch," he said in surly fashion. "What made you come to me about it, anyway?"

Dawkins was as tactful as he knew how—he had anticipated this question a month back.

"Used to be in the trade myself," he said. "I'm a third cousin or something of *the* Dawkins, but we had a row three years ago. Perhaps you heard about it? No? Anyway, if we hadn't had the row I'd have gone to him, but as it is I thought you'd be the best man for the business."

Mr. Carver was mollified, but his suspicions were still very acute.

"Where did you get all this stuff from, then?"

Dawkins in reply told him the truth. That was one of the best things about Dawkins' character. If there was only one course practicable, he took it without flinching and made the best of it.

"It's pirate treasure," he said calmly.

"What?"

"It's pirate treasure, just like the stuff you read about. We got it off an island in a small boat on the quiet."

Mr. Carver continued to make interrogative noises difficult to write in print.

"Of course," said Dawkins, putting his cards on the table with unembarrassed simplicity, "it was a bit of a steal. The government which owns the island—there is no need for you to know which— would want a good big slice of it if they ever heard about it. But it's months now since we got it away, and we know that they haven't heard a word. There'd been lots of unlucky searches for it before us—in fact we think there is one going on now. So it ought to be easy enough to get rid of it through quite ordinary channels. It's not as though it were modern stuff. No one except me and my partners knows what it is—police and people like that aren't on the lookout for it."

Mr. Carver was almost dumb for a moment, which just showed how much his emotions had been touched.

"Well," he said at length, "what—what *have* you got?"

"That's a good sample," said Dawkins, nodding at the diamond on the table. "There are about fifty as good as that. A couple of hundred a bit smaller. All sorts of cut and color. Some of it's old Indian stuff, as far as I can make out. You know the kind of thing—you find 'em on the market sometimes. They'll want recutting before they're any good for nowadays. People'll think some rajah or some one is getting rid of a bit of his stock. That's not a bad idea."

Deep need—and a pure artistic interest in addition—was making Dawkins positively eloquent.

"Besides that," went on Dawkins, "there's a couple of dozen uncut stones, big 'uns mainly, but God only knows what they're worth, I don't. And about twenty-five rubies—Burma, I think, and pretty good—and a few emeralds and some pretty poor turquoises."

Dawkins' eyes were fixed on Carver's face, and he could see the signs of a burning interest, despite all Carver's efforts to keep his features immobile. But Carver was still suspicious; he could not help thinking that all this might only be an ingenious plot to inveigle him into disposing for other people of property obtained in some fashion more criminal than that described.

"Let's see some more of them," he said.

Dawkins produced from his pocket another little parcel.

"There you are," he said. "That's one of the big uncut ones. And that's Indian, I think. So's that. That one isn't. And that's the best of the rubies."

Mr. Carver peered at the six stones which now lay before him. All of them seemed perfectly sound, and he could not recall any similar stones which had been stolen lately.

"D'you mind if I show 'em to one of my men?" he asked.

"Not a bit," said Dawkins. "But I wouldn't like 'em to go out of this room until we're more agreed about it."

Carver almost indicated approval as he picked up his desk telephone.

"Send Mr. Solomon to me," he snapped. "And bring me the trade list. You know the one I mean."

So did Dawkins. What Mr. Carver was asking for was the confidential list of stolen property circulated among merchants of precious stones, great and small.

The office boy came in with the list on the heels of Mr. Solomon. Mr. Carver's hand idly concealed the stones as he took the list, and remained there until the office boy had vanished. Not till then did Mr. Carver address Mr. Solomon.

"Here," he said. "I want you to look these things over. Get my instruments out of that case by the window there and find out all about them. Specific gravity and refractive index and all. Buck up."

Mr. Solomon bustled across to the window with the stones; Mr. Carver plunged into his confidential list; Mr. Dawkins leaned back in his chair, apparently calm but ready for anything. The room grew quieter and quieter, the silence only disturbed by the ticking of the clock and the slight noise made by Solomon as he fiddled with the jeweler's balance and the specific gravity liquids and the other instruments. Soon Solomon walked across and laid on Mr. Carver's desk one of the stones with a slip of paper.

"H'm," said Mr. Carver, reading the figures on it and clearly searching for confirmation in his list. The office boy brought in a card.

"Can't see him. Busy," said Mr. Carver. "Busy to everybody."

One by one Solomon brought back the stones and the figures obtained from them.

"Right. Thanks. That'll do," said Carver when the last stone had been weighed and measured and examined, and Solomon took his quiet way out of the room.

"D'you think I'm telling the truth now?" asked Dawkins.

Carver looked as if he did not, but he was nearly convinced by now that, truth or not, the business which Dawkins was offering him was not so entirely illegal as to be dangerous. He thought that perhaps, with a sufficient inducement, he might dabble in it. Should trouble develop he seemed to be sufficiently safeguarded to be able to prove innocence of intention.

"What are you offering me? Halves?" he asked.

"No," said Mr. Dawkins, and he said it in such a manner as to prohibit Mr. Carver entirely from expressing discontent at this flat contradiction.

"One-third commission. Thirty-three and one-third per cent. Three times the usual rate," said Mr. Dawkins. He had settled that mentally a long time ago. He did not much mind (such was his nature) whether he had a hundred thousand pounds or one hundred and fifty thousand, but all the same he disliked the idea of being robbed by Mr. Carver. The higher the rate of commission, the smaller the inducement to theft. And—this bulked large in Mr. Dawkins' mind—if he was able to show that he had paid Carver a larger commission than usual it would give Carver a motive for avoiding police attentions—such a suspicious circumstance would incriminate Carver as well, if any one were incriminated at all. And Dawkins, for all his apparent confidence, was not absolutely sure of his ground, although he knew— none better—that there was no mutual extradition treaty between Great Britain and the Rainless Republic, so that he was at least safe from Eguia.

Carver was thinking hard, too. One-third of a hundred and fifty thousand pounds was fifty thousand—quite a useful little bit. *And* there would be pickings, private rebates, as well. Business was slack, and the five thousand a year he earned was not nearly enough for his needs. There was, of course, something fishy about the business, but it might only be the fishiness of which Dawkins had told him. Certainly none of the gems shown him had any known history, so that he was covered from the law. And the fishier the business was, the less likely was Dawkins to complain about any of Carver's pickings and stealings, so that was all right.

"It'll take me a year, pretty nearly, to get rid of 'em all," said Mr. Carver, wavering.

"Nothing very surprising about that," answered Mr. Dawkins in complete agreement.

"Your partners likely to raise trouble at all?" asked Carver.

"No. Absolutely certain they won't," said Dawkins. "They don't know anything about this side of the business, and they've left it all to me."

"And where's the rest of the stuff?"

"In safe-deposit," said Mr. Dawkins, with his hand resting upon it.

"Well, tell me the name of this island you got 'em from."

"Not me," said Dawkins. "I've answered all the questions I'm going to this morning."

And with that the two men sat and looked each other up and down, one of them all a-flutter with the prospect of fifty thousand pounds' profit and fear of the unknown, the other expressionless, stupid and careless. Mr. Carver felt for an instant as if he were in the grip of one huge and soulless piece of machinery. Dawkins took a fresh grip on his hat and stick and gloves, and the gesture plunged Mr. Carver into a fresh fit of panic.

"Let's go over it again," said Mr. Carver desperately.

Then the haggling began; not haggling over the amount of the commission (Mr. Carver saw that it was futile to attempt to obtain more), but haggling over the terms of the agreement—indeed, Mr. Carver began by refusing to entertain the idea of any agreement and by expressing his dislike to putting anything on paper. But Dawkins insisted, with few words and no gestures, and against his immobility all Mr. Carver's impassioned gestures and unhappy rhetoric beat in vain. Mr. Carver in the end fell back upon the last resort of the weak; he asked for time to "think it over." Dawkins nearly yielded, but that strong sense of the matter of fact which enchained him recalled him to reality, and Mr. Carver, weak with emotion, gave in. A stenographer came in reply to Mr. Carver's pressing of a button, and retired with a shorthand script of an agreement between Mr. Adam Carver of the one part, and Mr. Henry Dawkins of the other part, regarding the supply and sale of precious stones. That done, Mr. Carver hardly noticed having to hand over to Mr. Dawkins two further documents—one a receipt for five diamonds, as listed, and one ruby, and the other a check for the not inconsiderable amount of one hundred pounds sterling, for which in return Dawkins gave his receipt, as an advance payment. Mr. Dawkins felt quite a little thrill as he folded up this last and put it in his pocket.

"Thank God I'm not a limited company," said Mr. Carver feebly, wiping his face with his handkerchief. "There'd be hell to pay with the auditors over this business if I were."

Mr. Dawkins said nothing at all.

CHAPTER IX

MR. DAWKINS experienced only a few hours' real activity after that interview for some days. He had to open a bank-account, put his jewels in a safe-deposit, buy himself a further supply of clothes, and establish himself in a hotel. Then at last he experienced a feeling of comparative ease and security; for the first time in fifteen weeks he was not carrying all those precious stones on his person. The first evening he dined leisurely and at ease, went to bed early and slept almost well. The second day dragged a little, and when the third came the novelty had entirely worn off. The fourth day was Sunday, and Sunday in a London hotel is enough to wring the soul of the most sedate of men should he be friendless. Mr. Dawkins obtained the exercise for which he craved by walking—walking unendingly round London streets, to Acton and Hampstead and Kennington and back again to a solitary meal at a lonely table in the gilded hotel restaurant. The drama had small appeal for him, and the silent drama less still. Dawkins drifted into and out of two or three theaters and cinematograph theaters in the course of each day, and it would be hard to say where he was most bored.

Small wonder, then, that the smiles of women in the streets seemed to become more vivid to him as he strode along, and small wonder that in the end one smile seemed more vivid still, and summoned Mr. Dawkins irresistibly, so that it was forty-eight hours before Mr. Dawkins returned to his hotel, without a penny in his pockets, his smart new clothes sadly rumpled and crumpled, and his eyes slightly bloodshot. Mr. Dawkins had crammed a great deal into those forty-eight hours, and Venus and Bacchus had presided over the cramming. He had done a good many foolish things, and said a great many more, although Mr. Dawkins, back in his hotel room with his head in his hands and a nasty pain in his head, could not remember very much about either. And for the life of him he could not account for more than a quarter of the thirty-two pounds he had had about his person before the plunge.

Mr. Dawkins began to feel the uselessness of

everything. A further interview with Mr. Carver, in reply to a telephone call from the latter, resulted in a fine large check to stiffen up a sadly flaccid bank-account, and a journey to the safe-deposit to obtain more stones for Mr. Carver to sell, but this hardly cheered Mr. Dawkins at all. Success and wealth were proving vastly uninteresting. Mr. Dawkins did not at all relish the prospect of spending the rest of his days in gilded boredom with nothing to do in a London hotel. What did rich men do when they had nothing to do? Mr. Dawkins asked himself this question in sternly logical fashion, and the answer came pat—they played games or they traveled. Dawkins had played Association football in his pawnbroker's assistant days, and in the army, but a man can't play football by himself. Travel? Paris, Italy, Jerusalem? Mr. Dawkins wrinkled his rather arrogant nose at the idea; in his disillusioned mood he strongly suspected that travel for him would be entirely comparable to his present existence in one spot. One idea, indeed, Mr. Dawkins turned over several times in his mind and left unadjudicated upon. That was to fit out an expedition to the Rainless Coast, beard President Eguia in his lair, shoot him if possible, and so fittingly avenge the death of the Hawk. At the memory of the Hawk the hard lines about Mr. Dawkins' mouth softened and hardened again, for he dearly loved the memory of that fiery little failure—a curious fact, but true.

But, Dawkins remembered, before he could set out on any of these schemes, he must go and hunt up Miss Royle, and tell her of her father's death, and see that all was well with her, just as he had promised the Hawk when he lay dying of starvation and gangrene in his arms. So far Dawkins had shirked this duty. He could not face having to tell a grave-eyed woman of her father's death— especially as a daughter must love the Hawk even more dearly than Dawkins himself did. And she must be pretty poor, too, Dawkins realized. The Hawk's silver mine had only begun to repay the money lavished upon it when Eguia seized it, and Dawkins was sure that the Hawk did not have a penny in the world beyond that.

It took Dawkins a whole day to nerve himself for the effort once he had decided upon it. He had his blue suit pressed and smartened by the hotel valet, and he paid very special attention to the brushing of his hair and the tying of his tie. Well groomed and bronzed, Mr. Dawkins was a very good example of the wealthy man-about-town as he set out for Norwood; he looked every day and more of his thirty-five years, but he felt that his appearance was such that he need not be ashamed of it, even before the Hawk's daughter.

Field Hill, Norwood, was easily found. So was number sixty-one. It was a tall thin house, badly in need, as were its neighbors, of repainting and repointing. Dawkins knocked upon the paint-blistered front door, and knocked again, and his knockings echoed cavernously within. He felt far less at ease than while swimming out among the sharks to wring the neck of Corporal Barroso.

The door was opened by a shabby little girl. Mr. Dawkins did not look at her particularly closely; he was not interested in little girls of ten with peaked white faces.

"Is Miss Royle at home?" asked Mr. Dawkins. The little girl did not seem to know of a Miss Royle.

"There's a Mrs. Royle," she said. "She's my— auntie. But she's out just now."

"Mrs. Royle?" said Dawkins blankly. This was

more than he had bargained for; he had come prepared for a daughter, but not for a wife as well; and he had always understood that the Hawk's wife was dead. And where was the daughter?

"No, it's Miss Royle I want," he said. "Is there one, or did one ever live here?"

The little girl smiled, and the smile lit up her peaked face. More than that; it sent a pang like fire through Mr. Dawkins' heart. For with the smile came a dazzling likeness to the long-dead Hawk.

"I'm the only Miss Royle who has ever lived here," said the little girl, vastly tickled at her promotion to "Miss Royle." Dawkins took off his hat and wiped his forehead, and as for words, they failed him entirely. The Miss Royle he was seeking, the daughter to whom he had come to pay his devoirs, was this frail, thin-faced, little girl in the shabby frock.

"Who—who else lives here?" stammered Dawkins, hot and uncomfortable.

"My grandma—at least, she's nearly my grandma. I call her auntie. And Charlie."

"Well," said Dawkins, rallying, "can I speak to —to auntie, then?"

"But she's out, you know. I told you. And I don't know how long she'll be. But of course you can come in and wait for her, if you like."

"Thank you," said Dawkins.

Dawkins sat in a ridiculous chair in a fluffy, ridiculous drawing-room, which, if Dawkins had had any eye for these things, he would have seen to be dusty and untidy. On the couch lay two or three open fashion-papers, and protruding from under the couch was a pair of down-at-heel, over-trodden pink slippers. But Dawkins saw none of this; his attention was too occupied by the small girl who sat opposite him on the edge of a chair, smiling shyly but inscrutably. Dawkins was never distinguished for his conversational powers, and he knew nothing whatever about children, so that he was feeling more awkward than his hostess. For a vague second he felt that instead of his fashionable blue suit and gray overcoat he ought to be back once more in an Eton collar and jacket at his first party; it took a glance at his fine clothes and a furtive touch at his pocketbook and check-book, emblems of power, in his breast pocket, to reassure him. He displayed a pathetic frankness.

"I'm awfully sorry," he said, "but I'm all mixed

up. I wish I knew who auntie was, and Charlie—didn't you call him?—and I don't know what your name is, although I've come all this way with a message about you."

"I'm Nina," said the little girl, "Nina Royle, and auntie is Mrs. Royle. She's my grandma, but I call her auntie. She's my father's stepmother, and when grandpa died she said I mustn't call her grannie any more, but auntie. And I don't know who Charlie is. He just lives here."

Even Dawkins' untuned ear could catch the bitterness in her voice as she said this.

"And what's the message you've brought about me?" asked Nina breathlessly.

"I'd better wait and tell auntie," said Dawkins, with fear in his heart.

"Auntie?" said Nina. "Auntie? She won't care, unless—unless—— Is it about daddy—about my father?"

"Yes," said Dawkins.

"Is he—is he——?" Nina's tone changed from hopefulness to dull despair as she saw the expression on Dawkins' face. "Oh, he's *dead*."

"Yes," said Dawkins, again, unhappily.

Nina's face twisted with woe, and her hands

tightened painfully. She slid from her chair and stood while the tears came, and then she came blindly forward to Dawkins' knee. He put a big arm clumsily round her frail little body, and she rested her head on his shoulder while she shook with sobs.

But the weeping did not last long. Soon she raised her head and dried her eyes with her handkerchief, and stood looking at Dawkins.

"Was it a long time ago?" she asked.

"Yes," said Dawkins. While on board the *Hammerfest* he had devised a good sentence, "His last words were about you," but it did not seem of use now.

And Nina stood and gazed at this big fair man with the worried expression; she was still racked now and again by a convulsive sob, and although she gazed at him she did not see him. It was only natural that, childlike, she should be full of her own misfortune and calculating the effect on her life of the death of her father whom she could hardly remember.

"I knew he was dead," said Nina. "That was why he never wrote to me and never came home to take me away from here. And I *did* want him to. I wanted him to take me away from auntie. And auntie was always saying that he didn't send any money to keep me, and she didn't see why she should, and I was no relation of hers. I used to think how lovely it would be if he came home suddenly and now—and now——"

The tears recommenced, and she leaned again upon Dawkins' shoulder. Dawkins put his arms about her, wrung with remorse, and too troubled to notice what he did. He lifted her featherweight on to his lap, and pulled his big linen handkerchief from his sleeve and dried her eyes.

"There. Sh!" said Dawkins, rocking her as if she were a baby; and his efforts to soothe her troubles were wonderfully successful. The tears ceased, and Nina found herself fingering the lapel of his coat quite calmly and interestedly. Now she began to notice how bright and fierce his eyes were, and how golden and silky was his little mustache. She settled herself more comfortably, curled up on his big knees, and smoothed back her tumbled black hair. She forgot her troubles in the arms of this very real protector, this big man (she was very conscious of his bulk and of the iron hardness of his muscles) with the hurt look, who had come from nowhere and taken her upon his lap. They had nothing whatever to say to each other, but that they did not mind. It was not for some time that conversation began to grow again, and it had hardly made a halting start before they heard a key in the front door, and voices.

"Here's auntie," said Nina, scrambling off Dawkins' lap and hurriedly trying to tidy herself.

Two people entered abruptly into the drawing-room. The first was a woman, short, stout and florid, overdressed, face painted, hair dyed (all these facts were evident even to Dawkins' eye) and withal conveying an impression of being slatternly—there were hints all over her of missing buttons and untied laces, although actually there was nothing as obvious as that about her untidiness. Trailing behind her came a gawky young man with a shambling step and shifting eye and a receding chin—Mr. Dawkins rightly set him down as the mysterious "Charlie" about whom Nina could offer such little information. The newcomers stopped short at sight of Mr. Dawkins' vast bulk rearing itself out of his chair, and Mrs. Royle's beady eyes ran hurriedly up and down him —took notice of the good clothes and the knife-edge trousers creases and the bronzed face and the gentlemanly mustache. There was an awkward pause. Then——

"I've come about Major Royle," said Dawkins.

"Oh, really? Won't you sit down, Mr.— er——?"

"Dawkins."

"Mr. Dawkins. *Mister* Dawkins? Light the gas, Charlie, and poke up the fire. Run down-stairs, Nina, that's a good girl. Run along, now, when you're told. Now, Nina——"

But Nina stood defiant, and edged back beside Dawkins' chair. So there they were, grouped at once into two hostile camps, Dawkins and Nina on one side, and Mrs. Royle with Charlie standing behind her chair on the other. Dawkins somehow guessed at once Charlie's position in the household —a passée widow and a young man with a shifty eye made the state of affairs evident; he had probably started as a lodger and eventually found a more economical solution of the problem of board.

"What is your news, Mr. Dawkins?" said Mrs. Royle icily, now. Her attitude had changed at once from flirtatious hospitality to guarded antagonism—goodness knows why, save that it was inevitable.

"Major Royle is dead, I suppose?" went on Mrs. Royle, noticing Dawkins' hesitation.

"Yes," said Dawkins. "He—died, nearly two years ago."

"I thought as much. And did he—is that precious silver mine of his, wherever it is, paying yet?"

"I believe so, but—there was a flaw in the agreement and it has reverted to the State."

That was putting it mildly, but Mr. Dawkins was in no mood for elaborate explanations.

"So that he left nothing?"

"Not as far as I am aware. But——" The "but" slipped out before Mr. Dawkins was ready for it. This was another of the scenes Mr. Dawkins had tried to visualize beforehand, over and over again.

"Well?"

"I promised him, before he died, to see that his daughter was provided for. He was the best friend I had."

Mr. Dawkins had actually come to believe both these statements.

"H'm," said Mrs. Royle comprehensively, and

she paused and looked up at Charlie. Then she continued cautiously, "I'm sure I've found keeping the child a very expensive business. You've no idea how much that child costs in food and clothes. And it's not as if she were any relation of mine. She's not my grandchild at all, of course. She would have gone to the workhouse if it hadn't been for me."

"It was very good of you, Mrs. Royle," said Dawkins. Mrs. Royle's hostility was obviously warring with the prospect of getting something out of a man so clearly moneyed. But a sharply drawn breath from Nina at his side told him that she at least was not in agreement.

"It's five years since Francis left her with me," went on Mrs. Royle, "and it's more than four since he sent me any money for her. That means an awful lot I've spent. And of course it will be more still now that she's getting older."

There was a light of greed in Mrs. Royle's eyes, and Charlie behind her was licking thin lips with a thin tongue. Dawkins saw it, and his loathing for the two of them roused him to deliberate action.

"I don't know who is the gentleman beside you,

Mrs. Royle," he said. "Has he anything to do with this business? It's private, you know."

"Oh, Charlie? He's all right, isn't he? He's——"

"He's not the person I'm here to do business with," said Dawkins heavily.

"But——"

"Look here, mister," said Charlie, "I'm here to look after Maggie's—Mrs. Royle's—business for 'er, and see that no one don't cheat 'er. See?"

Dawkins played the inevitable bluff, the trick which has succeeded ever since the stone age.

"Then that will be all," said Dawkins, standing up. "I won't try to cheat any one."

That put Mrs. Royle all in a flutter again.

"Oh, do sit down, Mr. Dawkins," she said. "Charlie, go away for a little while I talk this over with Mr. Dawkins. Go along now, there's a good boy."

Charlie went, muttering. But at the instant Mr. Dawkins had risen Nina had seized his hand in panic, clinging to it desperately. She was saying, "Don't go away, *please* don't go away," all the time that Charlie was being evicted; it was that which decided Mr. Dawkins on a new plan—a wild ridiculous scheme far madder than launching himself upon the Pacific in an open boat. He abandoned his original intention of merely trying to put the fear of God in Mrs. Royle. The twining of tiny fingers about his big ones settled it for him.

"Now see here, Mrs. Royle," said Dawkins, as soon as the door had closed behind Charlie, "I'm a rich man,"—it was the first time he had ever described himself as such,—"and I shall be spending the rest of my life in England. I think I shall be able to carry out Major Royle's wishes best by taking entire responsibility for Nina, here, and saving you any more trouble about her."

A convulsive clasp of the hands which held his told him that Nina had understood what he said and approved rapturously. Mrs. Royle looked at the pair of them; suspicion and relief and avarice and natural cross-grainedness all bore their part in her expression.

"What for?" she snapped. "Can't I look after her as well as anybody?"

"No," said Nina unexpectedly. "You know that——"

"Will you be quiet, you——?" said Mrs. Royle furiously, and then she stopped, realizing that this display of bad temper was as damaging, or more, to her argument as Nina's denial. There was a highly uncomfortable pause. Dawkins broke it.

"What about it, Nina?" he asked. "Would you like to come with me?"

"Yes," said Nina thankfully.

"That ought to settle it," said Dawkins to Mrs. Royle.

CHAPTER X

NINA had returned from school very unhappy. There was that in the attitude of her schoolfellows toward her which made her unhappy, although for the life of her she could not guess the reason for their sneers. She knew that it was something to do with auntie and Charlie, but Nina was not yet experienced enough to know that the relations between these two were such as to merit the disapprobation of the Puritanical tradespeople whose daughters composed the greater part of the school's pupils. Most of the daughters, it is true, hardly knew more than Nina, but they had guessed from the hints and nods exchanged by their elders that Nina was fair game for bad treatment, and with the cruelty of children they had turned upon her. The many weeks which had elapsed since the game had first started had not even yet begun to stale its novelty. Nina's puzzled little brain could not understand why she had suddenly become unpopular, and why there was even an altered tone in the mistresses' voices when they spoke to her. She came home alone, instead of with the half-dozen playmates who had once accompanied her.

The house was empty when she reached it, and there was no answer to her knock. That she was used to; she took the key from its hiding-place in the basement and opened the door for herself; the house was empty and desolate as a tomb, save where a fire smoldered behind its guard under a heap of slack. She sat down on the floor before it, gazing into its scanty rednesses, to wait until auntie and Charlie should see fit to come in. She was very, very lonely and unhappy—although at ten one hardly knows when one is unhappy if the unhappiness is not so great as to bring tears. She was not old enough yet to connect auntie's bad tempers with the days when her visits to the sideboard where the decanters were kept were more frequent than usual. All Nina knew about auntie's bad tempers was that they came and went, and that she was the sufferer from them. For if auntie tried to nag Charlie (as she did, sometimes) Charlie would growl something in reply and walk out of the house, and auntie would be worse than ever toward Nina. And hours afterward, when Nina was in bed, she would wake up and hear auntie and Charlie growling at each other down-stairs.

Charlie did not treat Nina so badly as auntie did sometimes, but for all that Nina disliked him more than she did auntie. She was vaguely conscious that he was an interloper and a sponger, and that his position in the house was doubtful; she hardly appreciated that even Charlie had vague troublings of conscience about this very matter, and that this was the reason for most of the snarlings and grumblings with which he treated her. He had struck her, too—only twice, but Nina remembered.

Nina was in the very act of conjuring up her usual day-dream, wherein a very handsome daddy (he was wonderfully handsome, but the cast of his features were prone to vary with Nina's light loves among butcher's boys and the like) would come knocking at the door, having sprung lightly from a crystal coach with six cream horses at the pavement's edge. And this handsome daddy would dress her in gold and jewels, and would bear her away to some land about which she felt necessarily vague, but which would be wholly delightful.

Nina, as has been said, was in the act of conjuring up this day-dream when Dawkins knocked at the door and the day-dream, after a disastrous beginning, started to come true. Nina held very tight to the big gentleman's hand; with a child's instinct she appreciated the changes of tension in the atmosphere during the interview with auntie; she exulted to the very depths of her when Charlie was made to slink from the room. She could feel that the big gentleman was poised and tense, and that he could wring Charlie's neck as easily as he could blow his nose. She felt her heart leap with joy and the lights turned into torrents of gold, and she felt deliciously warm and happy when the gentleman announced his intention of taking her away with him. She clung all the tighter to his hand and she could hardly keep still during the remainder of the interview, although long years of hard experience told her that it was always better to keep still when in the same room with auntie.

She sided with the big man during the argument like a wolf cub at its mother's shoulder. She dared auntie to her face, despite memories of ingenious canings and supperless bedtimes. In time she grew impatient with the argument. Auntie kept on hesitating and delaying, and the big man would not yield an inch. She could not quite follow the ins and outs of the matter, but there was that in the air which told her it was nearly settled when the big man put down a long thin book upon the table and ran his fingers through its pretty leaves, each decorated in fine purple ink and bearing a blue stamp. The big man asked for pen and ink, and she ran to her very own pencil box for a pen for him, and she found the ink-well, and brought them to the big man.

"Call that young man in now," said the big man, and she ran to the door and called "Charlie!" and Charlie came from his cave of Adullam in the basement. The big man was writing very carefully on one of the long slips with the purple ink, and when he had finished he tore the slip out and put the book back in his pocket, but he kept the loose slip close in front of him. Then he asked for paper, and Nina brought him some, and he set himself to further writing, very carefully, quite heedless of the new protests which Charlie was raising as auntie told him how far the argument had gone.

"There," said the big man, straightening his back and pushing the paper across the table. "You

sign that, Mrs. Royle, and *you*"—this to Charlie—
"can witness it."

Auntie and Charlie still tried to argue, but it
was clearly no use trying to argue with the big
man. As soon as he picked up the purple slip
again and began to put it in his pocket auntie took
hold of the pen and asked, "Where do I sign?"
The big man leaned across and showed her, and at
the same time he turned to Nina and said, "Run
and put your hat on."

And Nina ran, her heart singing and her legs
leaping. So little time was she gone that when she
returned the big man was just folding up the paper
auntie had signed and was putting it in his pocket.
Then the big man picked up his hat and smiled at
Nina—a funny, one-sided smile, but the nicest
smile Nina had seen for a long time, and Nina
smiled back, more of a laugh than a smile, she was
so happy. And auntie said:

"Oh, you can't take her like that, surely? What
about her things? Let me make up a little parcel."

And so they had to wait, with Nina dancing
with impatience, while auntie puffed up-stairs and
began to bustle about. But auntie came down soon
with an untidy brown paper parcel which was just

like auntie, and the big man took it and put it under his arm, and they went out through the front door and down the steps into the street where it was quite dark and smelled excitingly of fog, and the street lamps all down the road were points of light in a wonderful new world. And they went down the street and climbed on a bus, and the big man said, "Do you want to go on top?" and Nina said "Ooh, yes," and so they ran up-stairs and went to the very front seat, and the big man sat down with the parcel at his side while Nina stood up and peered over the front of the bus to look at everything, except when, at the moments of acuter realization of what was happening, she came back to the big man and tried to talk to him until she grew too excited to sit still and jumped up to look over the front of the bus again.

The big man, as a matter of fact, was not very talkative; he had a great deal to think about. Here he was with a child on his hands to look after. Although, curiously enough, that did not bother him much—he was too pleased at the prospect of companionship. What he was really wondering was whether there was any legal significance about the deed of adoption he had devised out of his own head and which Mrs. Royle had signed. Probably it had no value at all in a court of law, but Mrs. Royle had taken his check and it was hardly likely that she would give any trouble except for trying to get another check out of him. After all, she was quite right to be chary about handing the child over to the first stranger that came along—and the fact that she *had* done so in exchange for money went a long way to prove that she was unfitted for guardianship. The one thing that Dawkins, for some unknown reason, would not let his mind dwell upon was the astounding likeness between Nina and the Hawk as long as her face was not in repose. It made him uncomfortable, goodness knows why.

And Nina stood and watched the people, and the big, roaring, lighted tram-cars, while the bus thundered romantically onward, over a bridge across the gray river, and so on to a place where there were a myriad of the most intriguing flashing signs. Here the big man said, "Come on, Nina," and they plunged off the bus into the crowds on the pavement and Nina clutched very tightly his big horny hand. And they had hardly gone any distance when the big man stopped and struck his walking stick on the pavement and said:

"Great Scott, Nina! We've left your parcel behind."

So they stood for a minute wondering how they were to get it back, but the big man decided they could not just at present, and so they walked along through all the people and beside the dazzling shop-windows with Nina holding on to his hand saying over and over again in a happy dream:

"Of course it doesn't matter. Of *course* it doesn't matter."

Then they turned aside and reached a wonderful palace with shiny glass doors, which a wonderful man in uniform and two or three little boys sprang to open for them, standing at the salute as they passed through, to where there were lots and lots of lights and wonderful gold furniture and red velvet couches and marble walls. Here the big man stopped and talked to another man at a counter, and the other man looked at something in a book, and the big man wrote something down, and they talked a bit more, and then the big man said, "Come on, old lady," and she held on to his finger as they walked on into another little room full of mirrors which turned out to be a lift. Nina

knew *all* about lifts, of course, because she had
been in one before, but she couldn't help a little
squeak when this one started to go up because she
had never seen a little one like this before, nor one
so grand.

And the big man took her along a carpeted corridor to a bedroom with a lamp with a pink shade,
and he looked at her with a worried look and said:

"Better get your hat and coat off, I suppose. And
we'll have some tea. Would you like to have some
tea?"

And Nina said, "Ooh, yes," and when she had
taken off her hat they went down in the lift again
to a great big room full of white tables where the
roof was held up by pillars covered with gold, and
a band was playing, and lots of ladies and gentlemen were sitting at the tables. And a very polite
gentleman with a funny waistcoat came and
bowed to them when they sat down, and the big
man looked at Nina with his worried look and
said:

"What do you have at this time of day? Eggs
or something? And do you really have tea, or is
it hot milk or that sort of thing?"

And Nina said, "Oh, I *always* have tea, as long

as there's lots of milk in it. And I *do* have an egg, sometimes."

So the big man said something to the very polite gentleman, who hurried away, and Nina could then gaze round the room at the band and at the other ladies and gentlemen and at the big solemn face of the big man until the very polite gentleman came back in a hurry again waving a tray in the most wonderful fashion any one could possibly imagine, and he put down in front of the big man a whole lot of silver—teapot and milk jug and hot-water jug, and some cups and saucers, besides, and in front of Nina he put a dear little egg-cup with a nice fresh egg in it, and a plate of the loveliest thin brown bread and butter. And Nina ate her egg and drank the tea which the big man poured out with his brown hands that looked as if they ought to be clumsy but weren't, and she stared at him solemnly the whole time, but she was so excited she simply couldn't say anything until she had finished her egg, and then she was given a spoon and fork and a most delightful something on a plate that looked almost like two more eggs with cream over them until she started to eat it, when it broke up into fragments of sweetness and creaminess that melted in her mouth and were simply too delicious.

And when she had finished and wiped her mouth they left the table and went back in the lift to the bedroom with the pink lamp shade and the big man stood and looked at Nina more worriedly than ever.

"It's bedtime, now, Nina," he said, and he was so solemn as he said it that Nina might almost have felt afraid except that she knew there was nothing to feel afraid about while the big man was near her; and he went on to say, "But what you're going to sleep in now that we've lost your parcel I simply don't know."

And Nina said, "Ooh, supposing I slept in my combinations?"

And the big man said, "I suppose you'd better, old lady. We'll buy you some things to-morrow."

Then he went on looking worried, and he said, "Can you put yourself to bed?"

"Of course I can. I always do," said Nina. "If you come and tuck me up after."

"Righto, old lady," said the big man. "I'm just next door if you want me. Here's the wash basin.

You can see which is the hot tap and which is the cold tap. I'll come back in ten minutes."

And he went out quickly, while Nina washed her face and hands and pulled off her clothes and put them on a chair and scuttled into bed where there were nice clean sheets waiting for her which were very comfy although they were cold. And then the big man came back and said:

"Are you all right, old lady? Comfy?"

And Nina said, "Yes," sleepily, and held up her face to be kissed, just without thinking, and he kissed her, and drew the bed-clothes straight, and asked about the light, whether he should turn it out or not. And Nina said, "Yes," again sleepily, and so he turned out the light and went away very softly.

But it was not so nice when Nina woke up again in the dark and didn't know where she was. The room was so different from her own bedroom that she began to grow frightened in the darkness and called out. No one answered and she called out again, louder, and still no one answered. Then she was really frightened and began to cry and feel more unhappy than ever she had felt before, until she heard the door open and heard the big man's

voice asking softly what was the matter. And she
cried a little more until she felt the big man beside her, and she put up her arms round his neck.
And he lifted her out of bed and held her with his
great big arms so that she felt much safer than ever
she did on top of a bus. And he sat down on a
chair with her on his knee and lighted the gas fire
so that very comforting warmth spread over both
of them, and the room came to have just the right
amount of light in it. Then he said, "Half a minute, old lady," and put her down in the chair and
went away and came back again almost at once
with an overcoat with a nice fleecy lining which he
wrapped round her. Then he held her on his knee
beside the fire and didn't say anything much, but
he was just there with his big hard arms round her
while she became more and more comfy and happy
until at last she went off to sleep again on his
shoulder and didn't know anything more about
anything, not even about being put back into bed,
until she woke up again the next morning with the
daylight shining into the bedroom.

CHAPTER XI

DAWKINS' first experience as guardian of a little girl made a very big impression on him. He was far more embarrassed about things than was Nina, who took for granted a great deal which Dawkins only approached tentatively and after considerable thought. He had lost his heart to her from the very first, of course, and the memory of that first evening would, even years afterward, send a little warm tremor through him. He had hovered about the door of Nina's bedroom for long after she had gone to bed to make sure she was asleep, and when he came up again after dinner the pitiful little sounds he had heard from outside had brought him in in a terrible panic. He had gathered her into his arms in her ragged little combinations with a welling tenderness and gentleness which would have astonished Corporal Barroso, for instance, could he have looked down (or up, as the case might be) from whatever sphere to which Dawkins had dispatched him. He had sat by the fire with her in his arms for hours—for hours longer than was necessary, fiercely disregarding the cramps which assailed him and which wrung him with an agony worse than that he had known at the flogging post at Birds Island. After putting her back into bed— oh, so gently!—and going to bed himself he could hardly sleep for worry, and at five the next morning he was awake and up again, tiptoeing gingerly into her room to make sure she was all right. And the memory of that first kiss of hers, the free warm kiss of a little child, continually abode with him.

So that when Nina awoke after a sleep surprisingly sound despite its interval of fright she found herself smiling into the anxious blue eyes of Mr. Dawkins, who was bending over her, and she stretched and sighed with comfort under the warm bed-clothes like some small pussy-cat before a fire.

"Going to get up?" asked Mr. Dawkins.

"Ooh, yes, *rather!*" said Nina, with the prospect of another day of miracles before her.

It was Dawkins' brushes and comb which she used while dressing herself, and the chambermaid found her a new toothbrush (why is it hotels can always supply toothbrushes and never hot-water bottles?), and Dawkins wrapped his overcoat round her—shamefacedly, rather—and carried her across the corridor to the bathroom. Nina fully expected Dawkins to supervise her bath and toilet, and candidly was rather pleased at the prospect, but Dawkins simply could not. The sight of the Hawk's daughter in her combinations troubled his newly respectable soul to its depths, and he could not face the sight of her without them. It was a glowing, well-brushed, neat but shabby Nina who descended in the lift along with Dawkins at break-fast-time.

"The first thing we'd better do," said Dawkins, eating porridge, "is to get you some clothes and things, I suppose."

"Yes," said Nina fervently. It was a curious thing that she could not bear porridge while she lived at Field Hill, but here she was eating it with appetite opposite Dawkins.

"M'm," said Dawkins. "We ought to have a list. There's brushes and elastics and hair ribbons and goodness knows what. Do you wear hair rib-bons, old lady?"

"Of course not," said Nina, smoothing her shingled head.

"That's something," said Dawkins. "It'll be bad enough getting your clothes; but these other things will be simply awful. Let's write 'em down."

And in the intervals of eating bacon and toast the pair of them tried to make a list of the toilet accessories necessary to a young lady of ten, but it was not much use. Dawkins was simply hopeless, of course, and Nina, when it came to saying actually what she wanted, was not much better. Nina's wants were small, as a result of long years of doing without.

"We don't seem to be doing much good," said Dawkins pathetically. "I'm afraid we'll have to give it up and buy things as we find we need 'em."

That, however, was not necessary, as they were to find. They went out through the glass doors where the uniformed gentleman and the little boys sprang to attention, and walked sedately over to the big department stores which every woman knows and even men have heard of.

"This ought to do us," said Dawkins, throwing a guerrilla's lightning glance along the long line of windows. "They sell little girls' things here."

So in they went and were received by a morning-coated shop-walker.

"I want some things for this little girl here," began Dawkins.

"Misses' outfitting? Third floor. First lift," said the shop-walker, and to the lift they went, Dawkins feeling hopelessly conspicuous among the sparse early-morning shoppers, fur-coated women, all of them.

The lift shot them into the arms of another morning coat, and this morning coat piloted them over to a counter where they found peace in the charge of an exceptionally talented shop-girl. For this latter, as soon as she had pierced through Dawkins' embarrassment and ascertained that they wanted everything, *everything,* a young lady ought to have, and, seemingly, were not very particular about what they paid for it, rose splendidly to the occasion. She brought a list, which was sent to parents by one of the best girls' schools in England, of things which the girls had to have, and they worked through this, item by item, the shop assistant nonchalantly, Nina eagerly, and Dawkins sweating at every pore. At each item the shop assistant produced a selection of garments, and Dawkins would hurriedly order the correct number of the best priced ones, in a fashion strange to

Nina, who was accustomed to fingerings and mental figurings and prolonged debate. At intervals the assistant ran a tape measure over whatever part of Nina's anatomy was being clothed at the moment, while Nina put in a word here and there when her surprise permitted it. Drill dresses, for instance. Dawkins vaguely thought that drill dresses could wait for a while, seeing that Nina had no drill to attend, but the shop assistant, coldly, and Nina, excitedly, enlightened him to the fact that all self-respecting little girls wore drill dresses day in and day out. And underclothing. Dawkins, with his stone age knowledge of this sort of thing, thought that frilliness was a *sine qua non* of underclothing, and was surprised by Nina's repudiation of subsurface frilliness in any form, and by the shop assistant's support of her.

But when it came to party frocks the situation was rather reversed, for the arrival of a selection of party frocks was eagerly acclaimed by Nina but coldly regarded by Dawkins. For that sound common sense of his which was his only asset told him that the judgments of a little girl and of a shop assistant and of a mere man might all be at fault when it came to choosing party frocks. He would have preferred not to buy any at all, but Nina grew so woebegone at the disappointment, and the assistant's eyebrows rose to such a pitch that he gave way; but his common sense saw to it that only the two plainest and neatest frocks were bought. He was not going to run the risk of having Nina overdressed.

Hats were another source of trouble. Dawkins knew nothing at all about hats, and his brain whirled as he was led to where hundreds of hats awaited purchasers. But he stuck manfully to the same principle, and selected the plainest—and it was surprising what a difference it made to Nina to have her shabby old imitation velour replaced by a smart felt.

By the time that underclothes and stockings and hats and dresses had been bought, and shoes had been tried on, there was a mountainous pile of things on the counter waiting to be packed. Dawkins, with a glimmer of forethought, bought a couple of suitcases as well, before proceeding to the less prosaic domain wherein were to be found hair brushes and toilet-table apparatus—to which that invaluable list was still a guide.

And then at last the business was finished, and

the monstrous total added, and one of the store's messengers sent across to the bank with Mr. Dawkins' check to obtain cash to insure immediate delivery, and Mr. Dawkins himself sank back into a chair in the store's restaurant and ordered coffee, with milk and biscuits for Nina. He assured himself, as he sighed with fatigue, that he would rather spend a morning on Birds Island than one in a ladies' store, any day of the week. Then, with their purchases heaped into a taxicab (a new delight for Nina) they came back to the hotel, where the smart little boys jumped to relieve them of their burdens.

Dawkins surveyed the pile of parcels heaped up in Nina's room with trepidation.

"Are you sure you know what to do with all this?" he asked.

"Of course I am," said Nina.

"Well, we've got to do something with it," said Dawkins. "I suppose we'd better try to put it away."

Never was there such an untying of string and such a cutting off of labels, and such an opening and shutting of drawers. Dawkins had a twinkle of intuition.

"What are you going to put on now?" he asked.

"Ooh," said Nina.

The trim little hat and coat and neat frock which she put on during Dawkins' discreet retirement suited her marvelously—and they made her look more like *El Halcón* than ever. Dawkins caught his breath sharply as he came back into the room and saw the slight little figure in the middle of the room before the wardrobe mirror. He was quite embarrassed and uncomfortable about it. The thin face with the pointed chin, the firm lips and straight brows, the gray eyes and the black hair were the Hawk to the life. Dawkins stood stiff and silent while Nina preened herself in front of him.

"I *do* think I look nice," she said, "I do, really, don't I—er——"

They both realized the difficulty at the same moment.

"Do you know," said Nina, "I don't know what to call you?"

"That's so," said Dawkins.

"Of course," said Nina, "I could call you Mr. Dawkins, but I don't want to."

"Neither do I," said Dawkins. "You'd better think of something else."

"You know," said Nina, "you're just like my daddy. Shall I——"

"No, no, no, of course not," said Dawkins, horrified. The bare idea of comparing him to the Hawk seemed like blasphemy to him, and it was worse still that the Hawk's daughter should do the comparing. Dawkins did not fully realize that Nina's faint remembrance of her father (who had never paid much attention to her, anyway) was almost obliterated by her imaginings of him, and would soon be quite overlayed by her memories of Dawkins.

Nina was quite hurt by Dawkins' vehemence.

"All right then," she said reproachfully, "you choose, instead."

"Better call me uncle, I think, old lady," he said, full of contrition, and uncle it was. She tried it once or twice, tentatively, during lunch.

And at lunch further matters occupied Mr. Dawkins' mind. He knew absolutely nothing about the upbringing of children, beyond a vague idea that they ought to have plenty of milk and that they ought to sleep in the afternoon. This latter notion, of course, was laughed to scorn when he suggested it to her, cautiously.

"Why," she said, "I go to *school* in the afternoons, generally, so of *course* I can't go to bed then, can I?"

Dawkins could only agree and start a fresh line of thought on how to spend the afternoon. He fell back on the eternal resource of London uncles, brevet or otherwise.

"What about the zoo?" he asked, and Nina's face lit up with joy at the suggestion. She had never been to the zoo, she said, although all the other girls she knew had been (even Dawkins could gather from her expression the fact that the "other girls" had not been too kind about it, either) and she *did* so want to go. So the zoo it was, as soon as lunch was finished, with Dawkins' right forefinger tightly clutched in Nina's warm little paw.

"We've seen *everything*," said Nina, ecstatically to herself, as they saw the lions fed, and the sea-lions, and as she had rides on both the camel and the elephant. "I like the elephant best, I think, because the camel's nearly ugly." They had a wonderful tea together as it grew dark, smiling across the table at each other too happy even to talk, like the pair of children they were. And in the bus coming back Nina several times nearly went to sleep, and even Dawkins nodded now and then—what with shopping and the zoo and sleepless nights he was as tired as even Birds Island had made him. Nina went off to bed when they reached the hotel without a murmur, and when Dawkins came in to "tuck her in" she put up her arms to him and drew him eagerly down and kissed him with three big kisses because she was so happy. After that Dawkins spent the evening reading ponderously a book which had caught his eye on the bookstall in the hall—*The Management of Children*. Some of it was so far above Dawkins' head that he felt bewildered and inferior. He made a note, however, of the titles of several similar books advertised on the wrapper for future purchase and consumption, and made a dogged attempt to digest all the stuff about "the development of character" and so on.

That day established a precedent, and the four succeeding days passed in a similar swift and glorious panorama. They went to the Tower of London and St. Paul's and the British Museum and Westminster Abbey, and some of it they enjoyed and some of it bored them. And they wandered hand in hand round the Natural History Museum at South Kensington, and neither of them suspected that they were happy because they were together and had each of them some one to cherish. They ascribed their happiness, if either of them thought about it at all, to the museums and the churches. And in the evenings Mr. Dawkins toiled steadily through books on child management, scratching his head in bewilderment over Montessori, and musing over solemn translations from the German, and here and there gaining a gleam of light, but mostly working out his conclusions by the aid of his stolid common sense. The books gave him some useful data about diet and clothing which otherwise he could only have obtained by hard experience at Nina's expense: the sweet question, for instance. When Dawkins was a child, children were restricted regarding sweets because sugar was bad for the teeth. Dawkins now read (the theory was only contradicted in one of the books, and Dawkins weighed the evidence by the method of counting heads) that sugar never did any one's teeth any harm, but that sweets were deleterious because they necessitated eating between meals. All the books had something to say about eating between meals, and Dawkins' orderly mind thoroughly agreed with them. So that he kept Nina off sweets with what tact he could raise. It seemed rather hard on Nina, somehow. And he read about what a child ought to wear, and the evils of tight clothing (and he sought desperately in his mind for details of what he had bought that morning at the stores) and the right temperature of a child's bath (he bought a bath thermometer at the next opportunity) and how long a child ought to sleep, and what games a child ought to play, and what books a child ought to read (none of the authorities agreed with any other on these two points) and he frankly dodged reading the chapters about the Religion of a Child and about What a Child Ought to Know. At present he could not nerve himself to the consideration of these two matters, and his common sense was outraged at the oily emphasis which various books laid on them. The knowledge he was accumulating did not hinder him, fortunately, from seeing to it that Nina changed her clothes when they came in out of the rain dripping wet; that was quite an achievement.

But on the sixth morning Dawkins was embarrassed by the necessity of leaving Nina to look after herself while he attended to business. He did the best he could; he established her in a corner of the lounge with a pile of magazines from the bookstall, and he countered her promise to be good and not go away by his own that he would be as quick as possible, but his conscience troubled him deeply as he made his way to the safe-deposit for a further batch of precious stones and thence to Mr. Carver's office.

His conscience did not even cease from troubling him during the excitement of a duel with Carver. Carver was still suspicious about Dawkins and his diamonds, but his suspicion was gradually being allayed by the absence of difficulty in the disposing of them. Dawkins, on the other hand, did not trust Carver at all, and the interview was enlivened by Dawkins' demands to see checks and memoranda of sales. Carver found that Dawkins knew just as much as he did about secret commissions and private rebates (which, if Carver had known it, was not very surprising, seeing that Dawkins had left England under a cloud because of operations of this nature), and his commercial pride was touched at Dawkins' frank distrust of him as expressed by his refusal to let Carver have more than a few stones at a time. But in one respect the interview was eminently satisfactory for Dawkins came away with a check for nine thousand pounds and with the imminent prospect of receiving more yet.

Dawkins found that the possession of nine thousand pounds was, unexpectedly, curiously sobering, and it was a very thoughtful Dawkins who returned to the hotel where a very lonely and restless Nina awaited him in the desolate hotel lounge. All the decisions toward which he had been struggling so painfully lately came to him with a rush, even as Nina sprang from her chair and ran toward him. He sat down heavily beside her and characteristically plunged straight into the business. Frankness came more readily to him than the heavily rehearsed diplomacy with which he had encountered Mr. Simpson and Mr. Carver. He began to announce the conclusions reached during a whole series of thoughtful nights.

CHAPTER XII

"LOOK here, Nina," he said, "we've got to settle down."

Nina raised no objection at first; she waited for more details, so that Dawkins continued heavily with his plan.

"We've got to find a house," said Dawkins, "and furnish it, and we've got to find some one to look after you, a governess or something,—no, Nina, you mustn't make a face like that, old lady, —and you've got to go to school and we mustn't spend any more time just yet hanging about round hotels."

The expression "hotel children" was unknown to Dawkins, but his fumbling efforts at foresight had been successful inasmuch as they had called up before him a vision of what Nina might grow into if her present way of life were prolonged for a year or two.

"But why?" said Nina plaintively. "Why have we got to do all that? Why can't you look after me like you do now? I don't believe you want to."

Dawkins steeled himself against the disappointment in her pinched little face and sternly kept the argument on a prosaic level.

"Do you know, old lady," he said solemnly, "that I can be put in *prison* if I don't send you to school?"

"Ooh," said Nina. That made a difference.

"And if we don't have a house," he went on, "you'll have to go to a boarding-school, and then we won't see each other at all, not for months and months."

Nina did not notice the anxiety in Dawkins' blue eyes, for she was too busy with her own thoughts, but the anxiety was there right enough. The thought of losing Nina to a boarding-school after having so surprisingly won her was hateful to Dawkins, but—but—she might *want* to go.

"I wouldn't like that a bit," said Nina, to Dawkins' immense relief.

"Well, then," said Dawkins, "you see we've got to have a house, and find a school, and we'll have to find some sort of lady to look after the house for us, won't we, and see if your clothes want mending, and mine too, and all that sort of thing?"

"And what'll *you* do?" asked Nina.

"Me? Oh, I suppose I'll play golf."

Dawkins' tone was bleak and he felt a little lonely. He could only see an arid future of golf stretching illimitably before him. He could hardly bear to contemplate such a life of inaction, and yet if he were to stay where he could cherish Nina, and lead the respectable life he would have to lead if Nina were not to be gravely handicapped, he could not see how to occupy his time save with golf, which he had never played and for which he felt all the superior contempt usual in the lower middle class in which he had his origin. He had set aside his ambition to lead a filibustering expedition against Eguia; he had even set aside lingering thoughts of pretty ladies with vivid smiles. He was condemning himself, after full consideration, to a life of distasteful inertia, solely for the sake of Nina. And he did not want Nina to know he was making any sacrifice. Anxiously he eyed that small mortal across the table, where she sat considering things.

"Well," he said, "are we going to have this house?"

"Yes, of course," said Nina, and she forced a

smile. Somehow she did not want Dawkins to know that she was making a sacrifice in giving up the magic domain of hotels and the delights of sightseeing and her warm intimacy with Dawkins. He seemed so keen on the new program that out of love for him she yielded without a murmur— although her estimate of her own wishes and of the situation was much more a thing of intuition than of clear-cut consideration.

"And shall we have a house in London or in the country?" asked Dawkins.

"You choose," said Nina. She could not guess which he wanted and so she would not say.

"Sure you don't mind? Well, we'll live in the country, then."

And once these conclusions had been arrived at, the rest developed swiftly enough. That very afternoon found Dawkins and Nina together in a motor-car which bore them swiftly southwestward to where Dawkins had lingering memories of big green friendly downs, smooth and smiling and rounded—not scarped and jagged and inhospitable like the Andes. The country had changed somewhat since his boyhood; there were more houses and more roads, but the big downs were still there, bulking like friendly big brothers over the little houses at their feet. And these two wandered back and forth, finding a house for sale here and a house for sale there, and sometimes (for Nina, with Dawkins' finger firmly in her hand, this was a magical adventure) even going in and inspecting. Somehow it was wonderfully thrilling to go hand in hand with this nice man through empty houses which reechoed footfalls so curiously, saying, "This would be a nice room for you," or, "It's not a very nice view from here," and all that sort of thing, just as if they were both of them really and truly grown up. The gray evening was just beginning to fall when they reached the Other House (goodness only knew why it was called that, and the estate agent could never tell them) which sat beside a little lane just away from the main road, and seemed, as they neared it in the twilight, to open welcoming arms to them. Other minds might have thought it a very ordinary house, with its gray stone and white paint, save for great Summer Hill lying huge and magnificent just before it, and save for the little river, which, miraculously, ran through the garden and had to be crossed on a little white bridge.

Dawkins looked at Nina and Nina looked at Dawkins as they walked up the path, while the chauffeur yawned hugely in the car behind them. They both had the same sensation, although neither of them knew it of the other. This smiling gray house seemed to be welcoming them. Their footsteps on the gravel sounded somehow different, as they would sound were they at home, and the little river made its voice heard in the evening stillness to tell them that the house was not gaunt and dead, as had been the others they had visited, but warm and alive and kindly. Nina looked at Dawkins and Dawkins looked at Nina, and they walked round the outside of the house. Dawkins noticed that there were no neighboring houses; still they were comfortably near to the town; and there was no interruption of the view to the top of Summer Hill. He peered at the agent's list and saw that there was just the right number of rooms and all the amenities of civilization. He said just as though he were, against his own wish, denying to Nina some voiced desire of hers (although she had said nothing), "It's too dark to go inside, old lady. We'll come again soon," and they went back to London together, sitting very warm and close under the rugs at the back of the car.

Next morning, as though they were fearful of too much happiness, they turned their backs on Surrey and went away into Kent. But all the houses they saw there seemed ugly and angular, and the hills all seemed scarped instead of rounded. After an unkind lunch in a grim hotel Dawkins said to the chauffeur the word Nina had been waiting for, and they flew by crossroads into Surrey again and pulled up in the little yellow lane outside the Other House with its white gate and white bridge and green hedges.

And the inside of the Other House was just as nice as the outside. It was not a modern house—not aggressively modern—for the architect had not made the usual modern point of elimination of waste space and stairs. There was a long corridor up-stairs and another down-stairs, with awkward bends in them and with two steps down in each, very inconvenient for a carpet-sweeper, but homelike, somehow, and the front windows looked straight at the bulging chest of Summer Hill with its gorse bushes and heather. As far as Dawkins' unpractised eye could tell, the kitchens and pan-

tries and coal-cellar were practical enough—and if
not he could afford to spend money on them—and
the house itself was in good enough condition to
warrant preliminary inquiries and the outlay of a
surveyor's fee. He raised his eyebrows at Nina
as they stood and looked at each other in the bare
drawing-room where the wintry sun came through
the naked windows.

And Nina said, *"Yes.* Ooh, *yes."*

"Right you are, old lady," said Dawkins, "I
think we've got it this time."

Then they fled back to the agent's and Dawkins
took an option on the Other House, and finally
they reached the hotel with Nina's mind a pleasant
confusion of cupboards and staircases and white
bridges over little rivers.

Dawkins was perforce learning a great deal,
and his lessons recommenced as soon as the surveyor had announced that there was no radical
defect in the Other House—a decision which coin-
cided with the receipt by Dawkins of a check from
Mr. Carver for a further eight thousand pounds.
He wanted to furnish and decorate the Other
House, but he felt that he could not decide on
matters so important without skilled advice. A

preliminary inspection of showrooms convinced him that he was not competent to choose between oak and mahogany, and he had a vague idea that his taste in wall-papers would not be good enough to help establish the Hawk's daughter in the society which was her due. Furthermore, he wanted to learn to drive a motor-car (Dawkins had been sufficiently poor all his youth never to have acquired the art) and that meant leaving Nina alone for hours at a time, which he was unwilling to do. In the end a prolonged inspection of newspaper advertisements brought him into touch with the Dalton and Weston Agency.

Dawkins had a rough time explaining to Mrs. Weston, that stiff-collared, pince-nezed queen of scholastic agents, exactly what he wanted. He wanted a governess for a little girl—no, not his daughter, his adopted daughter. But he also wanted some one to help him choose the wall-paper and furniture of a house he was buying, and to engage servants for him, and supervise his housekeeping. No, he was not married.

"M'm," said Mrs. Weston. "And the little girl would be at home all day?"

"Well," said Dawkins, "I rather thought of

sending her to school after Christmas. Day school, only, that is. There is rather a good girls' school at——"

"M'm," said Mrs. Weston.

Mrs. Weston's basilisk glare through her pince-nez convinced Dawkins that he was asking a great deal, that he was asking the Agency to find him some one who would be hard to find—and that, of course, was just what Mrs. Weston wanted him to think. Dawkins felt hot under his collar, and he wriggled in his chair like some naughty little boy. Never before had he realized what a nasty piece of circumstantial evidence an adopted daughter could be. People simply didn't adopt daughters, unless they weren't all they should be. And Dawkins was further asking Mrs. Weston to find him a lady who would risk her maidenhood by living in the same house with him. He began to apologize for his very existence.

However, when at last Mrs. Weston had thoroughly brought Mr. Dawkins to heel (she had a little husband at home who bullied her, and she had to get her own back on the other sex somehow), she triumphantly vindicated the reputation of Dalton and Weston by producing Miss Lamb, whom Dawkins met by appointment at his second visit there and engaged thankfully, on the spot.

Miss Lamb was a Bachelor of Arts and a spinster of parts. She had taken her degree at London University some time last century and she held additional diplomas in Domestic Science and kindred subjects which fully entitled her to double the rôles of chatelaine and governess. She had taught at schools and in the houses of the rich; one of her pupils had since become a celebrated lady novelist, and a little boy she had taught had become a Member of Parliament, but a single interview with her would have absolved her, in anybody's judgment, of responsibility for either occurrence. She was a little fluttering woman, spectacled and tight waisted (there was a corset somewhere in the depths under that spotless blouse) and she fell in love with Dawkins on the spot. No man had ever wormed his way into the cloistered calmness of Miss Lamb's inner soul—no man had ever tried to. But the heart under Miss Lamb's pathetic, little, flat bosom beat quite rapidly as she regarded Dawkins' big muscular form in his blue suit, and his blue eyes and light hair with the golden lights in it, and his clipped mustache and the lines at the cor-

ners of his eyes and the flushed tan of his cheeks.
Dawkins always impressed women as seeming absurdly young, and flat-chested little Miss Lamb
straightway began to lavish on him the inexhaustible affection she had poured out all her life on
generation after generation of careless little in-
grates of one quarter his years.

Nina and Miss Lamb greeted each other coolly
enough at first. Nina only held in check her active
dislike of this interloper because she knew Mr.
Dawkins wanted her to put up with her, and she
did not want to bring back to Dawkins' mouth the
little hurt droop that showed so clearly when she
did anything he did not like. But later she grew
almost comradely over Miss Lamb's little enthusiasms, and having, with the aid of her diabolical
intuition, pierced Miss Lamb's fragile guard and
discovered her blossoming maidenly passion for
Mr. Dawkins, she gathered her into the broad-
minded toleration she reserved for people who did
not matter much one way or the other.

So Miss Lamb left, unregretting, the genteel
poverty of the gentlewomen's hostel where she had
been staying, and was installed in the Piccadilly
Palace Hotel in the next room to Nina's, and a sit-

ting-room was engaged where lessons took place each morning. Here for a week or two Nina did sums and made her acquaintance with the *First French Course* and struggled along the weary pathways of history and geography. But lessons, and walks in the park, even mealtimes, were very unimportant items of the day's proceedings. Far more exciting were the afternoon runs down to the Other House to see how the decorating was getting on, and whether the new garage was finished; and there were visits to furnishing shops, Nina, Miss Lamb and Dawkins altogether, where miles of carpets were unrolled for their inspection, and sideboards and armchairs and beds were debated upon. Miss Lamb had never been so excited before in all her life. From the age of twenty (and it would not be in good taste to point out how long ago that was) she had lived at schools and colleges and other people's houses, and now she was being given the deciding voice in planning a home of which she was to be the mistress. Her eyes were very bright behind her spectacles, but it was surprising how sharp those bright eyes were, and with what sound gentlewoman's taste she rejected the meretricious and the shoddy. Solid furniture Miss

Lamb insisted upon, but at the same time she would have it graceful of line and unassuming of appearance. Miss Lamb remembered with a shudder the mausoleum-like heaviness of the furnishings of some of the houses in which she had taught, and the brassy opulence of others. Mr. Dawkins, helplessly out of his depth, left things to her with an openly expressed gratitude that raised Miss Lamb to a seventh heaven of blushing pleasure.

In the evenings when Nina was in bed, and sometimes even, it is to be feared, while Nina was doing her lessons Miss Lamb was all a-flutter with lists and note-books, working things out in a hurried whisper to herself, for she found furnishing a house a big responsibility, and she had to think of everything, curtains and sheets and cups and saucers and coal-scuttles and dish-cloths, and holding a diploma in Domestic Science did not necessarily imply that she could not forget anything. It was all very exciting and delightful and frightening; and there were maids, too, to engage, two half-trained girls, because good servants would not bury themselves in the country.

But a fortnight before Christmas everything was ready, and Dawkins and Nina and Miss Lamb could drive down to the Other House in the motor-car Dawkins had just bought (power and promise of service and stiff price and lack of ostentation were its characteristics—Dawkins had watched Miss Lamb buying furniture) to supervise the assembling of the myriad things Dawkins had bought, and to wait anxiously to view the final result. And Dawkins saw that it was all good, from the light and airy dining-room to the pretty drawing-room and the solid furnishings of his "study," and his heart was glad within him, and Miss Lamb was very tired.

CHAPTER XIII

AWKINS had long ago foreseen what it was like to have a home. In his pawn-broker's-assistant days he had lived in lodgings, and even that period had been cut into unequal halves by his four years' war service, while since then had come the Hawk's campaign and the Birds Island interlude. He had never been the man of the house until now, and he savored the new conditions luxuriously. Once upon a time a word from him would swing a captive guerrilla spy kicking horribly at the end of a rope; nowadays he raised a dubious eyebrow at Miss Lamb at the other end of the breakfast table when the toast which Mary the parlor-maid brought in was soft instead of chippy. Instead of frantic thirty-mile marches, shoeless and starving, he now experienced idle walks through the dripping December fields with Nina prancing at his side. It was all different, and somehow he liked it. And the local bank manager greeted him with ever increasing respect as check after check came in from Mr. Carver and his holdings of gilt-edged securities steadily increased.

Dawkins, who had never planned before, spent his time planning nowadays. Long and anxious were the talks he had with Miss Lamb about Nina. Having no first-hand knowledge of children, he was compelled to fall back upon what the books said and what Miss Lamb could suggest. Many of the books waxed maudlin over the unhappy fate of the only child, and Dawkins swore grimly to himself that Nina should never go that way; that was why, with all due respect for Miss Lamb's teaching abilities, he determined to send Nina to the girls' day school at Gilding town. That would partly solve the problem—and he was too modest to realize that he himself supplied the remainder of the solution.

For Nina had never known such a splendid companion as Dawkins. He took everything very seriously, and he never laughed and spoiled it all— thanks to his atrophied sense of humor, although Nina did not realize this was the reason. He would talk about all the things Nina wanted to talk about, as equal to equal, and not as adult to child, or, worse, as adult-pretending-to-be-child. He could not do this last, for the simple reason that he could never pretend anything without a week or two to rehearse in. But he would back Nina up loyally in what she did or pretended, for loyalty to the family of Royle was grained into him. He would creep ponderously along hedges at Nina's heels, ambushing Indians or Germans as the whim took her, and he would take his part in extempore dramas (obeying dumbly and literally the fiercely whispered instructions she interspersed among her own speeches); in fact, he was as companionable and friendly and far more intelligent than any little girl could be. And he had attributes due to his position transcending any little girl's. He could stand up to irate keepers when they were caught trespassing, and he could carry her on his back across muddy stretches of lanes which otherwise would be impossible to her with the knowledge of an acute-eyed Miss Lamb waiting at home. He had a motor-car which could take them to places too far to reach by walking, and, once you were able to convince him of the urgency of the case, he could always produce silver to buy some vital accessory for drama or game.

That need to convince him kept them friends, curiously enough. For Dawkins had worked out in his mind how it was possible to spoil Nina, and he set himself resolutely not to spoil her. At cost of profound mental exertion he saw to it that he was not always relegated to a subordinate position in the dramas; he stood up manfully for his rights in the games they played; he would not gratify each and every one of her whims as they came along, much as it hurt him sometimes to give a refusal to her guileful pleadings. He reserved to himself the final decision in such cases, although, as Nina found, he was always willing to listen to the arguments she produced. In fact Nina, without noticing, discovered often enough that the search for reasons in her requests would find her wanting, and her whim flickered out for lack of unargumentative opposition. And Dawkins could stoop to cajolery on occasions, and once he had made his decision he was immovable. Dawkins, you see, had once held a high command in a guerrilla army, and there is not much difference between guerrillas and children, when all is said and done.

Those same guerrilla experiences of his, too, had taught him the evils of a divided command.

Nina's stocking (Nina put up with it; of course she was much too old to believe in Father Christmas or anything silly like that); and on Christmas morning Dawkins shamefacedly presented Miss Lamb with a five-pound note, which Miss Lamb accepted with joy in her heart, for her six months' unemployment before she attained this haven of rest had left her wardrobe very scanty even for a spinster of modest wants. And for three careless weeks after Christmas Nina and Dawkins spent their happy time together, until at last the first day of term dawned and after breakfast found Nina and him in the car together. Nina was bound for her first day at Gilding Girls' School, and Dawkins, a little self-conscious in his new plus-four suit (plus-fours were an object of derision to Dawkins when he was younger), was bound for his first lesson in golf from the Gilding town professional. For they had decided that every morning they would travel the two miles into town together, and in the afternoon Dawkins would fetch Nina if he were free, while otherwise she could take the local bus half-way home and be met (until she was more used to it) by Miss Lamb.

The club professional looked Mr. Dawkins up

and down, with an appreciative eye for his burly shoulders (in the neat brown suit made by the excellent tailor recommended to Dawkins by the Piccadilly Palace Hotel valet), for his powerful wrists and hands, and for the fierce determination of his craggy features.

"Ye say ye've never played before?" he asked.

"No," said Dawkins.

"And do ye just want to play, or do ye want to play *gowf?*"

"I want to be a good player, quick," said Dawkins sturdily.

"That's what I wanted to know. Ye've a weary way ahead of ye," grinned the professional. "Let's come and choose some clubs for ye."

The progress Mr. Dawkins made at golf, and his dogged determination and his unflinching continuous practise rather startled the golf professional more than once during the next three months. Golf, as golf, meant nothing to Mr. Dawkins; he was one of those rare mortals who remain adamant to the insidious charm of the game. All he wanted to do was to become a first-class player and so worm his way into Gilding society—he had decided that this was the readiest method, and having decided this his stubborn will carried him through. Six hours' practise a day and a great deal of thought—even such slow thought as Mr. Dawkins'—will work wonders, especially when backed up by Dawkins' giant strength. If Dawkins had ever been asked his opinion of golf, which he was not (the last thing one golfer would say to another is, "What do you think about golf?"), he would have replied, if he gave the matter due consideration, that it was a bit easier than digging phosphate but a bit harder than shoveling it. That is the only sort of opinion Dawkins ever held about golf.

So Dawkins practised his swing, and did approach shots by the dozen, and spent hours a day at the practise nets, and played rounds with the professional or his assistant, and said his first tentative good afternoons to other members in the club-house. The club professional, with a twinkle of humor, allowed him to play his first round with a fellow member in one of the monthly spoon competitions, where Dawkins mildly astonished his associates in the second division by winning easily and bringing his handicap down with a rush from twenty-four to seventeen. More people came to know Dawkins after that, and more people nodded to him in Gilding streets, and despite his rather reserved manner (Dawkins was a model of caution and patience, and, after all, he would not want to launch Nina into society for several years yet), he came gradually to be included in club-room conversations; and his opinion began to be listened to when he won the next month's spoon and brought his handicap down to twelve. Men would mention to one another, "That fellow Dawkins—don't know much about him, but he seems nice enough and he's dam' keen on golf." Those last words only serve to show how little they did know about Dawkins.

But by the time all this came to pass Nina's first term at school was finished and much water had flowed under bridges—especially along the little nameless brook which divided the garden of the Other House. That brook was a source of unending delight to Nina and Dawkins—although her first sight of it had given qualms to Miss Lamb, who darkly suspected it as likely to make the house damp and give everybody rheumatism. Nina, however, had developed a very specialized standard of regard for rivers. Just as Blücher exclaimed,

"What a city to sack!" when he first saw London, so would Nina, at this period, have exclaimed at sight of the Mississippi or the Amazon, "What a nice river to dam!" Damming the brook was a favorite pastime with Dawkins and Nina that spring. They would dabble about at its muddy sides with stones and clay, extending the dam feverishly when the spreading water threatened to turn its flanks, building hurriedly when the water rose over the top, and getting most gloriously wet and muddy in the process. Miss Lamb was inclined to condemn these pastimes, and her eyebrows would rise when Nina came pelting into the house cold and wet and daubed with clay, her hands (where they were visible) a fine shade of purple and her nose bright pink. But Miss Lamb knew that Mr. Dawkins saw no objection at all to any one getting wet and cold if there was a hot bath handy and plenty of dry clothes to change into, which was sensible of Dawkins, as even Miss Lamb, swamping her inherent Victorianism by her acquired Georgianism, came to admit. There was always great excitement over those Saturday-morning dams, especially at the great moment when lunch-time was near and the water was in consequence allowed to burst through the dam and come rushing in a tremendous torrent out of its deep pool and go swishing forward along its nearly dry bed, bearing with it its heap of accumulated débris. Nina nearly always chose that particular moment to lose her footing on a slippery stone and shoot down the bank in a sitting position into the six-inch deep water. Ooh, and it was cold! She had to run as hard as ever she could back to the house to the bath and the dry clothes whenever that happened.

During the weeks the craze lasted Nina looked forward to Saturday mornings even more than she did to Wednesday afternoons, which was the time for hockey. But the week-ends and mid-week were not (as even Nina would admit when pressed) so very much nicer than school-time. Gilding Girls' High School was a very much better place than the frowsy dame's school in South London to which her step-grandmother's snobbery (which sneered at Council Schools but sought out the cheapest of the other kind) had sent her. Nina did not appreciate it in so many words, but there is a world of difference between sitting at a badly made desk in a badly adapted, crowded room in a dwelling-house, and sitting at a respectable desk in a full-sized schoolroom with a sufficiency of windows. Sitting still was ever a trial to Nina—many were the "order marks" she received for wriggling—but the headmistress at Gilding had perhaps a little sympathy for little girls' wriggling, for either by accident or design the younger girls' classes were always arranged in the time-tables so that the next lesson took place in a room at the opposite end of the big building to the one in which the previous lesson had been given. And no time allowed for changing! Goodness, but at the end of the thirty-five-minute lesson how they had to run up the stairs and along the corridors! They would arrive all breathless—so much so that Nina would not start wanting to wriggle for the first quarter of an hour or so.

And when half-term arrived there was a new excitement to look forward to in the form of riding lessons in the riding school at Gilding; these, she knew, she owed to a suggestion from Miss Lamb, who at once sprang a good many degrees higher in her estimation. Indeed, it was not very long before Miss Lamb herself came riding with Nina, and although she rode with a side-saddle in a fashion which was hardly ever seen in Gilding she certainly could ride, as Nina willingly admitted. What was much more amazing to Nina was that Miss Lamb, when the color had been brought to her cheeks by a fast canter through the woods and over the hills, looked really pretty, with her eyes all shining behind the ugly thick spectacles.

For Miss Lamb was happier now than she had ever been in her unloved life. Many weary years of elementary mathematics and childish English made the running of a house sheer joy to her. It was an unspeakable, never-ending delight to walk round Gilding on Saturday morning with the tradesmen's books, mingling with the scores of opulent housewives similarly occupied, settling the weekly accounts and giving the weekly orders, having mid-morning coffee in Gilding's fashionable café, changing her books at the circulating library, and returning to a house where the servants carried out her instructions as a matter of course and not as a favor.

Between them they made an oddly assorted trio, did Dawkins and Nina and Miss Lamb, bound together in a powerful bond of happiness. And

Dawkins knew that the other two were happy, and on occasions was modestly amazed at such a definite success gained by himself, which went far to mitigate his first faint frettings at a life of idleness and ease.

CHAPTER XIV

MR. DAWKINS teed up his ball, took his stance, waited the split second he allowed himself for addressing the ball and then swung his driver in the powerful flat swing which the club professional had neatly substituted for his orginal pickax-like stroke. Those vast wrists of his took hold of the swing half-way through, and snapped the club through the top of the swing and the moment of impact, and carried it on over the follow-through, while the ball, cleanly hit with tremendous force, sailed up the fairway, pitched, ran and finally came to rest a useful ten yards on the hither side of the bunker which was designed for trapping weak second shots. It was a perfect drive, and the distance was extraordinarily good for a sodden course.

The Reverend Mr. Henry Gray raised his eyebrows a little.

"D'you do that often?" he asked. "You were introduced to me as a twelve handicap man, you know."

Dawkins would have shrugged his shoulders if such a gesture had been natural to him; as it was he merely looked awkward.

"Oh, well," said Gray, "let's see what I can do in reply."

Gray and Dawkins were beginning their first round together, on a week-day morning when the course was nearly empty. They had known each other by sight for some time, for Gray, being a clergyman, played his golf in mid-week, and had often noticed Dawkins toiling away in the practise nets or practising approach shots. Gray teed up his repainted ball, waggled carefully and drove his usual distance, comfortably on the fairway and fifty yards behind Dawkins. But his iron shot landed on the green, while Dawkins, who took his mashie, misjudged the strength slightly so that his ball rolled callously across and vanished into the pot bunker on the farther side. Dawkins' mashie brought it out again on the green, but the situation called for two putts, and as Gray took two as well, the hole was Gray's in bogey figures.

"Your honor," said Dawkins imperturbably, at the second tee.

It was a situation Gray had known often enough

before. He was used to being outdriven on occasions, but he could always rely on his approaching and putting to get him out of his difficulties, and his drives, although short, were consistently straight—which was more than could be said of those of most of the men he met. There was nothing spectacular about Gray's play; no mammoth drives, no holing of thirty-foot putts. But he was always down in two from thirty feet from the hole, and there were few opponents whom he met who were not worn down and heart-broken in the end by the machine-like regularity of his approaching and putting. Everybody knows the kind of golfer Gray was—it seems to be a specialty of clergymen.

It seemed, this time, however, as though the game were not to proceed on the lines to which Gray had grown accustomed. Lots of men would be upset at losing the first hole in that fashion after such a beautiful drive, and after only taking five for a hole with a difficult bogey of four. But Dawkins seemed quite unmoved and went on to the second hole not a bit downcast. Nor, on the other hand, did he seem at all elated when he won the long second, after another huge drive and a big

brassie shot had landed him on the green with
Gray an iron shot behind. Gray began to look
keenly at this burly fellow with the rather unintel-
ligent face. It was unusual to meet a man with a
complete lack of temperament—and Gray made a
study of temperament. He set himself doggedly
to play his best and try to wear down this immobile
opponent. Sooner or later those drives would be
sliced or pulled, and clearly Dawkins' approach
shots were not so good as his wooden club shots.
A prolonged sojourn in the fiendish rough of the
Gilding Club course might break this sturdy spirit.

That sojourn in the rough came inevitably, and
Dawkins' clumsy recovery lost him the hole in
question. But once again there was no sign of dis-
gruntlement on Dawkins' heavy features, and certainly there was no weakening in his play. He hit
his drives just as fiercely as before, fifty yards beyond Gray's best efforts. He approached just as
painstakingly and unfortunately. He putted with a
wooden regularity which matched Gray's own.
Gray began to tell himself, as half followed half,
that he must classify Dawkins' temperament as
genus novum. Also, he realized, he was playing
against a probable Open Championship competi-

tor of years to come. Another long hole was won by Dawkins, and they were all square again, but into Dawkins' flinty blue eyes there came no gleam of hope, no hint of elation. Gray found himself more puzzled than ever. He rather specialized in men (that was part of his job) and this was a new type to him. But all the same he did not think too hard about it, for he wanted to win, and concentration was an essential ingredient in the recipe of victory.

They came to the up-hill eighteenth, all square still. It was a wickedly difficult hole, dog-legged and littered with traps for the unwary. Mr. Gray was full of hope, and his hope increased as he saw from Dawkins' stance that he was setting himself for the long and difficult carry across the angle.

Dawkins' driver hit the ball with a clean hard smack, and if Mr. Gray had been of a despondent nature his hope would have welled out of him as he saw the ball tower over the rough and drop just upon the fairway. As it was the spectacle only filled him with a grimmer resolution as he played his safe short drive to the near fairway. Mr. Gray's brassie shot was one to be pleased about, for it skipped fortunately over the turf quite a long way up the slope beyond which was the green. Dawkins took his iron, but was unlucky, possibly in encountering heavier going, for his ball came to rest alongside his opponent's. Mr. Gray took his mashie from his bag with pleasurable anticipation. A forty-yard mashie shot up-hill to an unseen hole would be a hard trial to such an inexperienced golfer as Dawkins, good though he was. Mr. Gray's mashie clipped through beautifully, and the ball soared up-hill and dropped over the ridge to Gray's intense delight; he knew from experience that it would stop a few feet at most from the pin. Dawkins said not a word; he grimly took his mashie and his stance, and in his usual cold-blooded fashion played his shot after the barest possible consideration. Wordless they walked up the slope together. Some of the men Gray knew would have chattered nervously, with a, "Good match, this," or, "I wonder where we'll be on the green," and others would have been sullenly bad-tempered over Gray's fortunate second shot and their own unlucky one. Dawkins, on the other hand, was neither pleased nor sorry; he was neither excited nor ostentatiously indifferent—there is a very subtle difference between Mr. Dawkins' kind of indifference and the usual golfing indifference.

And on the green, when they climbed the ridge, lay the sight which Mr. Gray, judging by the flight of the balls, had expected. Glistening white upon the green they lay, one two feet from the hole— that was Gray's, and another on the edge of the green, forty-five feet away; that was Dawkins'. Mr. Gray was more pleased at the proof of his judgment than at his certainty of victory; his conscience pricked him a little regarding his two lucky shots. But Mr. Dawkins had taken his putter from his bag and was striding over to where lay his ball. Mr. Gray hastened to remove the flag from the hole, full of consideration for so fine a fighter. Mr. Dawkins ran an eagle blue eye over the undulations of the green. He scanned the line and judged the distance in one sweeping glance. He struck his ball solidly, neither tentatively nor desperately, and it rolled forward like destiny over the folds of the green. Onward and ever onward, until it struck the back of the hole with a satisfying thump and clattered to the bottom of the tin. Mr. Gray, flabbergasted, tore his eyes away from the hole and looked across at Mr. Dawkins—and Dawkins was putting his club back into his bag.

Even in his present startled state of mind Gray
made two instant deductions from this fact. Dawkins must have begun to put back his putter
before the ball reached the hole. That showed
that, to say the least, he had not followed the
course of the ball with all his heart and soul. Also
it showed that as soon as he had struck the ball he
had known that at any rate it would stop nearer the
hole than Gray's—no one human could have pre-
dicted for certain its going in, even then. The one
deduction proved that Dawkins' indifference was
not assumed, and the other that he had a solid
confidence in his putting, quite justified by his
achievements during the round, and was an additional proof that the result was not quite such a
fluke as it might appear at first sight.

Concentration notwithstanding, Gray found it
impossible to sweep all these thoughts from his
mind as he applied himself to the putt necessary to
halve the hole and the match. And even as he addressed the ball a new deduction came surging into
his mind with such clarity and rapidity that he
could not check it in time to save his stroke. He
remembered the woodenness of Dawkins' expression, and his apparent carelessness about the result.

Gray realized, in that clairvoyant flash, that this carelessness was not only apparent, it was real. Dawkins simply did not care whether he won or not. He was not really interested in golf. But all Gray's clairvoyance could not inform him why a man not interested in golf should practise it for six hours a day. Thoughts of this kind are not conducive to good putting. The rush of realization had come just as Gray drew back his putter for the stroke, and the inevitable result was a weak-minded twitch of the club and a stabbing shot which sent the ball gaily past the lip of the hole and a yard beyond. Gray had lost the round and Dawkins had won it. Gray's study of the golfing temperament of his opponent had for once in a way cost him a new ball.

It was not until a fortnight later, after they had played two more rounds together, that Gray, having confirmed all his deductions by further close observations, began to act on them. They were lunching together in the club-house after the round.

"Golf's a fascinating game, isn't it?" began Gray Jesuitically.

"Yes," said Dawkins.

"It doesn't leave you any time for anything else, does it?"

"Not if you want to be any good at it," said Dawkins cautiously. There was a twinkle in Gray's eyes which warned him to be careful, and so he tried to draw farther into his shell than ever, and to make only a sparing use of the clear-cut English he was acquiring by painful observation of Miss Lamb.

"And some us are *desperately* keen on being good at it, aren't we?" laughed Gray, and Dawkins grew restless and uncomfortable. He guessed that Gray had realized how uninterested he was in golf, and with his social future at stake he was going to take no chances. Otherwise where would be that respectable golfing guardian he visualized for Nina, and the friends he hoped to win for her? He put down his knife and fork and eyed Gray straightly across the table, with his hands hard clenched beneath it. Gray, accustomed to dealing with men's souls, noted the gesture.

"I don't want to rag you," he said, suddenly serious. "I'm desperately earnest. Do you mind?"

"Of course not," said Dawkins, relaxing. He

liked Gray—who, by the way, was the only parson he had ever met socially in his life.

"Well," said Gray, oddly embarrassed, "it—it's not easy to begin. But I've seen you playing golf, and I've seen you practising golf, and—and—hang it all, man, you know what I mean. And you can't guess how I covet the time and the thought you spend on the game. To me they'd be worth—well, I can't tell you what they'd be worth, because I couldn't measure them by material values."

"I'm sorry," said Dawkins still carefully, "but I'm afraid I don't quite understand."

There was a trace of a flush on Gray's cheeks, and he was speaking with the vehemence of sincerity.

"Confound it!" he said, "you've no idea what a handicap it is being a parson. I have to be on the watch all the time in case I start preaching. And I spend half my time with dear old ladies who are ready to take anything I say for Gospel. It's a dreadful handicap when one has to talk to a man. But—oh, let's come down to brass tacks—how does the idea of good works appeal to you?"

"Good works?" asked Dawkins vaguely, rubbing the back of his head.

"Yes. Visiting the poor, and all that sort of thing. You don't believe in God, do you? I didn't think you did—men with your look in their faces never do. I don't even want to ask you to try to. It wouldn't be fair. It's not your soul I want to badger you about. It's the rest of you that I covet."

Dawkins liked sincerity in a man.

"Well," said Gray, "shall I go on, or shall I run for my train? Have you had enough already?"

"Oh, go on," said Dawkins, and Gray resumed with more self-control.

"It's like this," he said. "I work in London all the week, except on Tuesday mornings when I come down here to play golf. I'm an organizer in a mission, and I'm the one lone male among a heap of women. Some women are jolly good, and all my lot are as sincere as—as—is the devil sincere? I suppose he is. But they're only women, when all is said and done. The young varsity men I get who come down to go missioning aren't the best kind of varsity men—at least not one in a hundred is. You know the kind of young man who goes in for settlement work. Sometimes he's hysterical and sometimes he's inquisitive, and nearly always he

takes an unhealthy interest in religion. Oh, you
know what I mean. It *is* unhealthy for a young
man to worry about vestments and predestination.
I want a man who isn't a parson, and who doesn't
care tuppence about the souls of the people he's
talking to, and who doesn't know an alb from a
chasuble. And I want him to *work*.

"You've got money in your pocket and you'd
give me some if I asked for it, and it would be
useful, but it wouldn't be nearly so useful as your
time. I can get money any day of the week from
fat sentimental women in the West End. But I
can't get good men anywhere. And I want 'em—
oh, so badly. There are people to visit and data
to collect—some of my women can do that pretty
well, but they're all overworked—and there are
swarms of boys and girls and young men to talk
to and feed if necessary and encourage. It's no
good worrying them about their sins if their bellies
are empty and they've lost their nerve.

"And the kids! I know you're interested in kids
—you see I made careful inquiries about you before I talked to you about this. You ought to see
ours—four hundred or so of 'em. The women all
want to teach 'em how to play brainy games and

that sort of thing, and I can't stop 'em. I'm paid for that, too, if it comes to that, by my never-sufficiently-blessed trustees. What I want is a sane sensible man with no theories and a lot of sense, to do anything that wants doing barring preaching, to come along one or two days a week and an evening or two as well, perhaps. Well? Yes or no? Or do you want to think it over?"

"I don't want to think it over," said Dawkins. "I'll come."

Dawkins was terribly tired of golf and he liked Gray; and he had begun to chafe against inaction. And although his prejudices instinctively reacted against the idea of "good works," the thought of having something definite to do was positively grateful to him.

That was Dawkins' introduction to settlement work in the East End. He was a strange fish out of water there, among earnest young men and curate-worshiping young women. His grim face and his good clothes marked him out from his fellow workers, and he was conscious of his oddness in that environment, but he stood it out. He embarrassed the young women who talked theories to him by his complete ignorance of theories; he shocked the young men when unguarded conversation proved his ignorance of highly important tenets of the Christian religion—he was once even betrayed into asking whether a certain Dean was a Church of England man or a supporter of the Congregational mission round the corner.

But he did his work. His feats of brute strength in the gymnasium amazed all the slouching youths who came, and brought them back again next time with their friends. His beautiful motor-car, crammed with children, was to be seen nosing its way out through the suburbs in search of fresh air and a glimpse of the sea. Sometimes a hectic little party after a frantically exciting afternoon on Summer Hill would come back to the Other House for tea served by an exquisite Miss Lamb with the assistance of a decorous Nina in the background. When information had to be gathered in some especially unpleasant spot, or from particularly recalcitrant parents, it was Dawkins who was charged with the duty. His huge frame and smart clothes were in time quite well known in some of the more filthy blocks of tenements out Limehouse way. He learned to draw the necessary nice distinction between orderly disorderly houses and disorderly orderly houses, and there were times when the blazing wrath in his eyes effected what the pleadings and threats of the authorities had been unable to effect. It was not long before he made his one creative suggestion, whereby he employed for fortnightly stretches unemployed hobbledehoys from the settlement about his garden and garage. A fortnight of good food and spoiling by the maids, with just enough pottering work to keep them busy, and money in their pockets when they returned worked wonders with a good many of the slouching youths. The garden was not in Dawkins' province; he had handed that over to Miss Lamb, who supervised its welfare as much as Harris, the daily gardener, would allow her to, and it is to be feared that the youths' efforts were not of much use nor very welcome to either of them. But there was weeding and lawn-mowing to do; and it is rather to be fancied that Miss Lamb kept one special bed solely to be dug and redug by each new protégé in turn. Dawkins found them car-washing and metal-polishing in plenty, and the experiment was successful from the start. As Mr. Gray said, a thousand men like Dawkins would solve all the problems of the settlement.

It is not to be imagined that Dawkins enjoyed his work at the settlement. He just did it and felt most uncomfortable in the doing of it because he had learned by experience that he had to have something to do to keep his mind occupied—and he found next that he was beginning to enjoy his golf on the days when the settlement and Nina between them allowed him time to play. Incidentally, as soon as that happened, his phenomenal rate of improvement slowed down considerably— Dawkins was not such a good player when he wanted to win. But he was growing popular among his fellow members.

CHAPTER XV

THE Easter holidays at Gilding Girls' High School came and went, spring changed gradually and perfectly into summer, and Nina and Mr. Dawkins grew steadily closer together. It was a queer bond which united those two, the more especially as it was largely wordless. Dawkins would hear from Nina, bit by bit, all the tale of her naughtinesses at school; he would share her indignation at some outrageous whim of one of the mistresses. Nina even brought to him her difficulties in her home work, despite the fact that Miss Lamb was in the house for that special purpose.

Dawkins came in time to expect and desire her knock upon his "study" door and the sight of her thin face (not so thin now, and with freckles here and there) looking round the corner to see whether his six hours' golf had caused him to nod himself to sleep in the big leather armchair. She would climb up into the companion armchair on the

187

other side of the fireplace and stare at him seriously as he puzzled over whatever difficulty she had brought him. Twenty years ago Dawkins had had a good secondary school education—than which England can provide no better, nor the whole world show—but he had since then done his best to forget it, and now he had to begin all over again. It was odd to see him knotting his brow over the elementary geometry and French which Nina brought him. He would puzzle and ponder and frown—he had never been blessed with the mental agility elementary problems call for—but at last he would break through to the light.

"See here, old lady," he would say, "you remember——"

Dawkins had always to go back to the solid first principles, for he had forgotten the later dodges and formulæ, and he would work out the problem starting from initial axioms—and that, of course, was very good for Nina. They would worry it out between them, and Nina would trot off at last with something more solidly grained into her. Some of her work, botany for instance, was quite new to Dawkins, and because of her he had to learn all sorts of new things about calyx and corolla, stamens and pistils, so that before long he had for his own sake to take an interest in the garden which Miss Lamb cherished so tenderly. Until then Dawkins hardly knew a carnation from a dahlia.

Dawkins and Nina were learning other things besides school work. That Easter holiday they found out all sorts of things about England which they did not know before. From Gilding in its eligible situation in the heart of Surrey they pushed out in all directions, partly by car and partly, because Dawkins became cramped and fidgety in a car, on foot. They early discovered the glory of Hindhead and all the North Downs which heaved up their big green bulks about Gilding. They wandered round Winchester and they climbed the campanile of Chichester Cathedral. One never-to-be-forgotten day, after some intensive map reading by Dawkins, they penetrated into the hardly traveled area northwest of Arundel, where the huge downs, with scarcely a sign of humanity to be found on their high ridges, stretch in a vast bulk out to Petersfield. On one of those summits they sat for a whole glorious afternoon, with Mr. Dawkins luxuriating in the green splendor of the Weald, with its little red villages and white lanes spread out before them, while Nina was so filled with the beauty of it all and so exhilarated by the wind which blew past their ears that she could only hug herself round her stomach and say, "Oh, golly! Oh, golly!"—an expression of which Miss Lamb disapproved but which alone expressed her emotions adequately. Dawkins would freely have given all the Andes, from Panama to Patagonia, for those ten miles of downs between Petersfield and Arundel—and he could hardly be called a sentimentalist.

Then there were the rivers—the Wey at Guildford and Godalming, and a little venture or two upon the Thames, and, of course, experiments with their very own baby river in the garden. Dawkins and Nina were both of them examples of the very common type for whom running water is an irresistible attraction. They were always building dams or sailing toy boats or rowing real ones.

One Saturday morning occurred the Great Adventure; Easter holidays were over and summer was fairly come. The preceding night, after Nina had gone to bed, Dawkins had arrived from London in the car, with a huge parcel at the back. So far he had said no word about it to Nina, and the parcel remained in the garage, but at breakfast he wriggled restlessly in his seat and could hardly eat any food, and kept looking at Nina's plate to see when she had finished. The moment the last bit was eaten and Miss Lamb had given her permission to leave the table, Dawkins pushed his chair back, too.

"Come on, old lady," he said, "I've something to show you."

And Nina took his hand and they dashed out into the garden and round the corner to the garage and there beside the car was a most beautiful little boat, at the sight of which Nina could only clasp her hands and gasp. It was a collapsible canvas boat, so small that it hardly seemed big enough for Nina, but Dawkins assured her that it would carry both of them easily, thanks to its air-pockets round the gunwale—"And it will, too." And there were two little oars which could be used as oars or paddles or could be screwed together to make a double paddle.

"We can find out now what lies beyond the ditch," said Dawkins.

For although they knew the course of the little river all the way to Gilding where it ran into the Wey, they knew nothing about it above the Other House, because the banks there were interrupted by big ditches, and there were plowed fields to negotiate, and when they had tried to strike across the river from the road higher up they had been held up by barbed wire and notice boards and had never succeeded in penetrating through to the waterside, especially as it seemed that the river curved away from the road higher up. The source of the river, in fact, was as great a mystery as the source of the Nile once had been, and the two of them had often debated about it. Dawkins had religiously kept his eyes off that part of the ordnance map where the mystery would have been unromantically explained—his purchase of the portable boat had not been entirely spontaneous.

"M'm," said Dawkins, "do we want hats? Don't think we do—do you, old lady? I thought not. But we want soft shoes. Let's see who's ready first."

Nina was ready first, of course, and she simply danced with impatience when Dawkins remembered something else and had to go back to the house again. But he was soon back, and between them they lifted the boat and carried it down under the little bridge and put it in the water, and it floated beautifully. Then Nina got in, so gently but so excitedly, and Dawkins lowered his huge bulk gingerly into the boat too. Nina had to sit between his knees. They each took a paddle and were off. And they looked out up the high green bank as they came out from under the bridge, and Miss Lamb was there in her coverall with her gloves on all ready for a busy hour in the garden, and Harris the gardener was there, and the new boy from London, and they stood and watched them as they made their way, rather uncertainly, against the moderate current up toward the unknown.

They were not very good at it at first, because in places the water was not deep enough for them to paddle and they had to push against the bottom with the paddles instead, and they were not very used to it at present, and the river wound about so. But they learned quickly enough, and went on up the stream, sometimes with fields at the top of the banks at either hand, and sometimes with trees overhanging the water. At one place where the bank had given way a little there was a cow drinking with her fore feet in the water and her hind legs high up the bank in a remarkable attitude, and she was very surprised when the green boat shot round the corner close upon her.

"Fancy being wrecked on a cow!" said Nina.

But that indignity was spared them, for the cow, with a snort of surprise, heaved herself up the bank again and eyed them suspiciously as they went by. They pushed on steadily, following curve after curve of the river until Nina had quite lost her sense of direction. The sun climbed higher and higher overhead, and it grew hotter and hotter—the first really hot day of the summer, and the sky was blue and the grass was green and the trees were shady, and Nina, pottering away with her paddle (any one can guess who supplied most of the motive power) was as happy as a queen. The river was like a stream of diamonds and sapphires; liquid jewels dropped from Nina's paddle as she lifted it from the water. Then they passed from sunlight into the dense shadow of a wood through which the little river wound a tortuous way.

To Dawkins, laboring in the stern, the sudden twilight and the stillness brought a whole rush of dark memories. For the moment he was not in England with Nina, but instead he was in the Andean foot-hills, admiral once more of the Hawk's canoe navy on the Rainless Lake. Dimly in front of him he could see the laboring shoulders of Joaquin, the Mosquito Indian (how he had strayed from the Caribbean to the Rainless Coast was a puzzle), the finest canoeman in the country. Out across the little bay along whose edge they were paddling so cautiously was moored the terrible new motor-boat which Eguia at incredible cost of blood and treasure had brought up and launched upon the lake. Yesterday it had hunted down the canoes, spitting death from its machine-guns, leaving their riven hulks drifting amid a tangle of twisted bodies. One more day like that would see the command of the lake pass from the Hawk to Eguia, and that would be the beginning of the end. It was Dawkins' duty to lead his last canoes under cover of night and capture the motor-boat by boarding. It was the last throw of the dice, the last effort left to the henchmen of the Hawk.

The paddles were dipping silently, and they were creeping along without a sound. Dawkins, peering through the twilight, could just make out the loom of the motor-boat in the middle of the bay. He steadied the canoe on a fresh course toward her, and he could sense a corresponding change of direction in the rest of the little fleet, as they swung out from the shadow of the shore on to the open water. And then hell broke loose in a flash. A dazzling searchlight from the boat clove the twilight, and the machine-guns began their infernal loud-voiced chattering. Joaquin fell dead across Dawkins' feet, the canoe lurched and swayed, bullets whipped the water to right and to left. Some one in another canoe screamed horribly. Dawkins set his teeth and lunged fiercely with his paddle in a mad effort to close with the clamorous motor-boat. But the hail of bullets tore through the sides of the canoe and flicked out the brains of the last two paddlers. There was a lurch as the canoe fell over and the water closed round Dawkins and the icy pang (for the lake was fed from the snow-covered Andes) seemed to sear him with pain as he swam blindly in the glare of the light. As he reached welcome darkness once more he could just make out the dim forms of two last canoes lurching toward the shore and safety.

Then came the swim to shore, and the desperate

crawl past the outposts of Eguia's land forces as
the dawn caught the summits of the Cordilleras,
and at noon he reached the camp of the Hawk and
told him the dread news of the shattered navy and
the ruined cause. And the Hawk had almost
blanched before his fierce rage took hold of him
again, and he issued the orders for the starving re-
treat which led him to two more battles, defeat,
gangrene and death. Dawkins shuddered and
writhed in his nightmare.

"Ooh, we nearly went over then," said Nina,
and the nightmare fell from Dawkins like a veil as
they shot out once more into sunlight.

Dawkins blinked happily up at the blue sky and
drank the air of an English summer with huge
gulps of relief.

CHAPTER XVI

THEY came to a place where hurdles were laid across the stream, and the bottom was rocky, and they had to climb out. Dawkins took off his shoes and stockings, and so did Nina, but in addition Nina tucked her diminutive frock inside her other things, and felt much happier in consequence. The banks were not negotiable, so that Dawkins had to exert all his giant strength and lift the boat over the high hurdle while standing in two feet of water, and then they climbed after it and resumed their progress. Neither of them mentioned to the other the need to put on their shoes and stockings again; they were both of them far too comfortable. And Dawkins did not have the heart to tell Nina to pull her frock out again, although his conscience assured him that Miss Lamb would most certainly disapprove.

A little way farther on Dawkins drew the boat in to the grassy bank.

"Do you know what the time is, old lady?" he asked.

"Oh, about ten."

"It's nearly one."

"Goodness! What about dinner? Whatever will Miss Lamb say? And I *am* so hungry."

Dawkins stepped, with surprising delicacy for one of his bulk, out on to the bank and looked at Nina's worried little face.

"Come and sit beside me," he said, "and I'll tell you something. And I'll show you something."

As Nina scrambled to his side he began dragging parcels out of the bulging pockets of his plus-four jacket.

"Sandwiches," he said. "Apples and oranges. Hard-boiled eggs. Careful with that, that's milk for you. And that's something else for me. You see, I remembered to tell Miss Lamb that we wouldn't be back for lunch, old lady. Something told me we wouldn't."

Nina kicked out her bare legs luxuriously in the sunshine, and rubbed her cheek against his rough sleeve.

"Of course it did," she said, and she meant it.

Despite the size and number of Dawkins' parcels they were all of them empty soon enough, so that Nina sighed happily and rolled over on to her side, and Dawkins stretched himself on the flat of his back with his arms behind his head and a cigarette in his mouth and contemplated the blue of the sky with silent satisfaction. It was quite half an hour before Nina's insatiable restlessness reasserted itself and she sat up and joggled Dawkins.

"Come and see what's round the bend," said Nina. "And we haven't found out anything about the source of the river yet."

It was that suggestion about seeing "what was round the bend," of course, which lured Dawkins on; and Nina, being feminine, had known as much. They worked their way steadily up-stream, with heaps of incidents now. Time and again there were hurdles to lift the boat over, and once or twice there were shallows they had to wade past, towing the boat. Luckily the boat unladen hardly drew an inch of water. There was always the excitement of seeing what awaited them round the next bend, and thanks to the height of the banks they neither of them had any idea where they were. Now and again they would climb up to the top and look round. Usually there were cows to be seen, and sometimes sheep, and very occasionally some one could be seen working in the fields. They were in a fold in the ground at the foot of a steep ridge, and a long way away they could still see Summer Hill, the last and greatest of the ridge, and they knew that the Other House was in that direction in consequence. As though it were a hundred miles away they could just hear the noise of the Saturday-afternoon traffic on the main road right across the valley, but it only served to remind them that they were out of the world in the heart of a haunted fairy-land. The shadows were very long before Dawkins could bring himself again to say that they ought to be going home.

"It's been *such* a lovely day," said Nina. "I don't want to leave it all. I don't. I don't."

"But we won't get home to-night if we don't start now," said Dawkins, feeling just the same. For the moment his comfortable house and his attentive servants had no attraction for him at all. Then a sudden idea struck him.

"By George!" said Dawkins, "we *won't* go home to-night, either. Shall we have an adventure, old lady?"

Nina looked up at Dawkins with the bursting

admiration a child displays for an adult who says the right thing. Dawkins' resolve crystallized hard and firm, and he put aside his fear of Miss Lamb and his new-grown respect for the conventions.

"Come on, old lady," he said. "Tie the boat up here. Good and tight, mind, so that it'll stay till we get back."

They tied the boat up securely to a bush, and climbed up the bank. At the top Dawkins looked round him with a guerrilla's eyes.

"This way, old lady," he decided. "Over this field and the next one. Through that gap, and if there isn't a lane there you can call me silly. And that lane will bring us to a village, and there is always a shop in every village."

Mrs. Timmins, unsuspecting behind the counter of the General Stores, Post-Office, Grocer and Italian Warehouseman, had a series of surprises that evening quite unexpectedly. The Saturday-afternoon business had ended, and there was a lull before the last comers were due—the slack and careless individuals among the village housewives. Then the shop-bell jangled, and two people came in; one was a big bronzed gentleman in brown plus-fours and the other was a little girl. The big bronzed gentleman began buying all sorts of things, bacon and eggs and bread and butter and a little frying-pan—that one'll do—and a kettle and tea and sugar and tomatoes and a tin of milk, and do you sell blankets?

"Well, sir, I do."

"Good, we'll have some. Doesn't matter much about the color. Those four'll do. And macintosh sheets?"

"I'm sorry, sir. Don't keep those."

"Well, what have you got? Tarpaulin? Sticky stuff. Here, what are those hanging up there? Macintoshes? Let's have a couple, big ones."

Mrs. Timmins could not help uttering a protest. It seemed a scandalous waste of money to buy macintoshes when obviously there was no intention of wearing them.

"They're thirty shillings each, sir."

"That's all right. Put 'em in with the other things. Anything else? Forks? Plates? I suppose we'd better, hadn't we, Nina? A couple of those forks and three tin plates. That ought to be the lot. What's that, Nina? Good for you, old lady. Yes, we want some cups. Not tin ones. Hate 'em. Two of those china ones. You can carry those, Nina, along with the eggs. Stick the rest of the stuff in a sack or something, if you don't mind. Oh, and after all I think we'll have a yard or two of that tarpaulin. I beg your pardon? Oh, yes, a rick-cloth would be just the thing. Stick it in the sack. I'll use the telephone if you don't mind while you put 'em away and add up the bill."

Dawkins never told Nina what he said when he telephoned to the Other House. Truth to tell, he was a little nervous about breaking the news to Miss Lamb that he and Nina were proposing to spend a night together without a roof over them. It was this nervousness which accounted for his unwonted garrulousness while buying the stores, and it simply redoubled itself when he lifted the receiver and asked for the number of the Other House.

"Is that you, Mary? I want you to take a message for Miss Lamb. . . . No, *don't* go and call her. I—I can't stop. Just tell Miss Lamb that Miss Nina and I won't be in to dinner—in fact we won't be back at all to-night. . . . Yes, that's right. We won't be back until to-morrow, lunch-time, perhaps. . . . Right. Good-by."

He came out of the box to where Mrs. Timmins

and Nina were stuffing the last of the purchases into the sack. There was quite a crowd in the shop now.

"That's seven pounds one and fourpence, sir," said Mrs. Timmins apologetically. That was about as much as she took in the whole of some Saturdays, but Mrs. Timmins was not the kind to be elated about it.

Dawkins tugged out his pocketbook and paid her—it is symptomatic of newly acquired wealth to carry large sums in cash—and then he stooped over the bulging sack. Mrs. Timmins wanted to help him with it, but he twitched it dexterously to his shoulder without an effort. There was not much left for him to learn about carrying sacks. He bowed his back to pass under the low door of the shop, with Nina at his heels, leaving an amazed shopful of people behind him. At the village pump he stopped and pulled from his pockets the milk bottle and his whisky flask for Nina to fill along with the kettle, and then they passed on out of the village into the growing twilight.

"Which way now, old lady?" asked Dawkins, and of course Nina did not know. One gap in a hedge was very like any other gap to her, especially when presented another way round and in a different light. Nina could no more have found her way back to the boat than she could have flown there, and she realized it. But Dawkins knew quite a lot about Nina by now, just as he knew a lot about guerrilla troops, and he made no attempt to rub the lesson in—which was as well, because Nina would have resented it. He just swung round into one of the fields and headed across it, and Nina loved him for it. It was only a few minutes before they were back by the little river again, and Dawkins could put the sack down.

"M'm," said Dawkins, "we'll want a fire first, I suppose."

Nina was simply thrilled at the idea of a campfire. Dawkins produced his pocket knife and walked back toward the hedge.

"Shan't be long, old lady," he said, nor was he. He was back almost at once with an armful of dead wood he had cut from the hedge.

"That's ready when we want it," he said. "Tent's the next thing, isn't it?"

Nina did not know; it was all too delightful.

Dawkins opened the sack.

"Put the stores over on that side, old lady," he

said. He laid the macintoshes on the empty sack and the blankets on the macintoshes and unfolded the rick-cover and mused over it for a moment.

"Easy as anything," he said. He brought the boat paddles and dug little holes in the ground so that they could stand in them blade upward. He tied one edge of the rick-cover to them, and Nina held each one up in turn while he ran round with string and pegs made from forked sticks and guyed them securely. Then he pegged out the opposite edge of the rick-cover, and then the sides, and behold, the rick-cover had become a neat wedge-shaped tent open along one side between the paddles.

"Now you'll be all right even if it rains, old lady,—which it won't," said Dawkins. "Let's have some supper now. We've earned it."

He built up a little handful of fire, carefully but rapidly, in the lee of the tent opening.

"Don't know whose land we're on," he said. "We'll get run in for trespassing or something, perhaps, if any one sees us, so we don't want a big blaze. Besides, we can cook much more easily on a small fire."

So it seemed. In less time than she would ever

have thought possible (save that she was too excited and happy to think anything impossible)
Nina was sitting on the pile of bedding eating
bacon and eggs and bread and butter, and drinking tea with condensed milk (which she hated
normally, but which tasted heaps nicer than ordinary tea when drunk out in the open with a
hint of beautifully smelling wood smoke in her
nostrils). She ate and ate until she was as tight as
a drum and most marvelously happy. The fire had
died down to red embers, the stars had come out,
all the noises of the night had crept in round them,
and the river was gurgling and chuckling in a way
she had not realized it did until this evening
silence came. And she was very tired with all her
paddling and walking and excitement, and Dawkins was very near and reliable. She wanted to
stay awake and enjoy it all and go on enjoying it,
and the more she wanted to keep awake the drow-
sier she became, so that she found herself drooping
on to Dawkins' big firm shoulder and he put his
arm gingerly round her and held her carefully for
a little while,—because he wanted the evening to
go on for ever, too,—but he soon stirred and remembered his duty, and said:

"Bed, old lady?"

And Nina said, "Ooh, no," but she was too tired really to mean it, so Dawkins picked her up and sat her on the sack while he spread the macintoshes over the floor of the tent and took one blanket and doubled it neatly for a ground blanket. Then he said:

"It's like that first night, isn't it, old lady? You'll have to sleep in—some of your clothes again. Miss Lamb wouldn't like it, and neither do I very much, but it can't be helped this time, can it?"

And Nina said very sleepily, "I haven't got any combinations on to-day. Shall I wear my vest and knickers?"

"Yes, that'll do," said Dawkins hurriedly, and he walked nervously away while Nina got ready.

You see Nina was eleven now, not merely ten, and Dawkins felt more awkward even than he did before. But she was soon ready, and Dawkins came back and showed her how to fold her blankets under her and over her, and he reached down and doubled the tail up under her feet so that she was wrapped up as if she were in a cocoon and warm and comfortable and without much chance of kicking the blankets off during the night. Then he made up a little pillow for her under the ground blanket and spread his handkerchief over it so that the roughness of the wool would not irritate her face, and she snuggled down happily. Then just as she was going to sleep she remembered.

"Aren't you going to sleep in the tent, too?" she asked, in such a drowsy voice.

"Not just now," said Dawkins in his comfortable voice, ever so far away. "I'll be all right, old lady. Good night."

"Good night, daddy," said Nina.

It is too much to guess whether Nina said that last word after careful consideration or whether it just slipped out. For by now her vague memory of her father was quite blotted out by the continual presence of a miraculous but reassuringly human Dawkins. Dawkins had done all and more than she expected a father to do—as far as Nina knew a father was a kindly person who took her away from auntie and fed and clothed her and helped her with her home work—to say nothing of taking her for marvelous journeys up rivers, and cooking exciting suppers over camp-fires, and building providential tents.

But that little word made Dawkins jump in his seat on the sack at the tent mouth with the blood running hot under his skin. It would have been a pleasant, yearned-for sensation if only he had not felt at the same time a horrible feeling of treachery and disloyalty toward the Hawk. He sat very still for a while, a prey to a mixture of conflicting sensations. It dawned upon him that Nina had never used the name "uncle" toward him after the first two or three tentative tries at the Piccadilly Palace Hotel. From what Dawkins knew of Nina (and that, by now, was a great deal) she had set her heart upon calling him "daddy" and had worked steadily to this end. Dawkins was torn between his own desires and his love for Nina on the one hand, and his loyalty to the memory of the Hawk on the other. And Nina, snuggled down under blankets under the windbreak of the tent, smiled in her sleep out of sheer happiness. Owls flapped by in the darkness, and screeched and hooted far worse than ever they did at the Other House, so that the noise was heard by Nina even while she slept, but it did not trouble her sleep, for she had lain down secure in the knowledge that Dawkins was close at hand.

Dawkins, indeed, sat patient and still until he was sure that Nina was asleep; so still in fact that the little night wind which came breathing over the fields found him cold and set him shivering. He reached for the one blanket he had kept for himself and put it on in the old fashion he had learned on the Rainless Coast. With his pocket knife he cut a small slit in the center of the blanket, passed his head through and drew the edges beneath him as he squatted on the empty sack with his knees up to his chin. That was how his guerrilla Indians had slept, and he had learned the convenient trick after much trial—it was far and away the most economical use of a single blanket. Clasping his knees, he gazed, solemn and a little melancholy, into the night. He was happy enough, but a whole train of somber thoughts dragged through his mind as he squatted there.

Boyhood memories, even, of his school, and of his lodgings when he had begun to learn the business of pawnbroking; of nights in France—of one night in particular in High Wood when Platoon Sergeant H. Dawkins had distinguished himself sufficiently to earn a D.C.M.; of the agony of his journey from the aid-post back to the field ambulance after that fragment of shell hit him in the side; of the long and wearisome convalescence in England, after they had cleared the wound of sepsis and taken out those torturing drainage tubes; of the months and months after that in a training camp in England, drilling more and more infantry to feed the furnaces at Passchendaele and Cambrai; of his passage back to France during the German offensive; of the evidence he had had to give (a bitter memory, this) at the court-martial which sent a man to his death; of his practically compulsory transference to an Officer Cadet Battalion, so that only the Armistice stopped him from holding the king's commission. Then demobilization and a resumption of pawnbroking, with tiny pay and squalid lodgings, so that it was almost inevitable that, infected as he was by the constant example of the evasion and subterfuge of army life, he should turn a listening ear to the temptations of that thieving fellow clerk who needed a confederate—and a catspaw. Dawkins remembered the stammering volubility of his Jewish employer when discovery dawned upon him, the hysterical gesticulations and venomous threats, dying down when he saw Dawkins' fists clench. Then the passage to Callao, and the beach-combing and general loafing before he strayed into the army of the Hawk.

Now he was back; he had a vast and growing bank balance, and investments in War Loan, and a house and ease and leisure—so much leisure that he had had to find voluntary work for himself. And, truth to tell, Dawkins found not very much pleasure in these things. Success was rather flat and stale to him. All his happiness now was bound up in the hands of the little girl sleeping back there in the tent. There had been a lapse or two from virtue since the mammoth debauch which had preceded his visit to Field Hill, but the memory of them had slipped from Dawkins' mind without leaving a trace. He could hardly remember the features of any of those frail women of the night. They had had no share of any of the passion he cherished for little Nina, there; and that was a passion so powerful that his stern common sense compelled him to keep it in check lest it should harm its object, and kept him thinking steadily of means by which he could give Nina all she needed or wanted without her feeling that all she ever needed or wanted was coming her way. At least three-quarters of Dawkins' thoughts were directed

to that end. And so they were to-night, until at
last, despite want of practise, his forehead drooped
down upon his knees, and he slept, like an Indian,
for the few hours before dawn.

Before Nina woke Dawkins ran heavily back
to the village to obtain more drinking water, for
he would not trust the water of the stream, and by
the time Nina began to wonder in puzzled fashion
where she was he had all the ingredients for breakfast ready to hand and firewood cut. She came out
of the open mouth of the tent blinking at the
strange new world; two fields away a colony of
rooks had just arrived and were beginning a tremendous powwow about the day's work, and the
dew was on the grass and the hedges, and the little
morning mist, presage of another scorching day,
had not yet been dispelled. Dawkins in some odd
way was quite embarrassed at sight of Nina in her
artless attire, and he averted his eyes as he suggested that she wash and pointed to the stream.

"There's no soap," said Nina.

"Doesn't matter," said Dawkins.

"And no towel."

"Use the clean hankie I gave you for a pillow-
slip last night."

Nina washed, kneeling at the water's edge, filling her hands with the clear cold water and splashing it excitingly over her face and neck. She was a pretty picture in her boyish clothes, with her thin shapely arms coming out of her white vest and ending in sunburned boyish hands.

When she came back Dawkins had just poured the boiling water into the teapot and was cracking eggs into a spluttering frying-pan. And the odor which arose from that frying-pan was simply heavenly. Nina ate bacon and eggs with barbaric appetite, and drank great cups of tea, and secured more than her fair share of bread and butter. She felt deliciously savage as she looked across to where Dawkins was busy with knife and fork, with his hair tousled and a ferocious potential beard sprouting over his sun-scorched cheeks. She loved him then for the set of his heavy shoulders, and the vigor of the glance of his blue eyes, and his big, dexterous, square hands. Nina was just reaching the age when people were becoming a combination of details to her instead of a blurred complete effect, and the change did not diminish the favor Dawkins found in her eyes. But then he had the advantage of a good start.

After breakfast Dawkins regarded Nina with a hint of trouble in his face.

"I don't know what Miss Lamb will say to us when we get home, old lady," he said. "We oughtn't to have done it, you know."

"No," said Nina, "but I don't think she'll mind very much when we tell her what a good time we've had together—daddy."

Their eyes met across the dying fire, and in that very second the name question was settled once and for all.

"I suppose now we've got to go home," said Nina plaintively, "and we haven't discovered the source of the river even now. I don't *want* to go home."

Dawkins brought a campaigner's mind to bear on the subject. He knew that although they were seven hours from home by water, they were not more than two hours by road—and that two hours might cut down to twenty minutes if they could find a motor-car anywhere. He put forward a suggestion which brought the light back into Nina's eyes, and ten minutes afterward, with the sack of stores cached under a hedge, they were pushing on up-stream again in the boat.

That was how it happened that an hour later a certain Eminent Gentleman walking round his marvelous garden in the freshness of the morning (most of his week-end guests were just beginning to think about breakfast) saw a tiny green boat suddenly shoot out on to his lake. When they saw him beside the water the occupants clearly hesitated; then they decided to make the best of it and drew into the bank where he stood. The Eminent Gentleman looked at them curiously. One of them was a burly figure in an expensive but bedraggled plus-fours suit, terminating comically in bare legs, and the other was a small girl who might have been nondescript were it not for the keenness and acuteness of her features. She, too, was barelegged (and more than that) and bedraggled—no one would believe what a time the two had had getting the boat over little weirs and up little waterfalls.

"Good morning," said the Eminent Gentleman.

"Good morning," said the little girl. The man was rather too conscious of trespassing and intrusion to say anything. "We're exploring."

"That's more than most people ever think of doing," said the Eminent Gentleman.

"Yes," said the little girl. "We started yesterday, and we haven't been home all night. We're looking for the source of the river."

"I'm afraid you've found it at last," said the Eminent Gentleman. "I'm sorry."

His voice reechoed sympathetically the disappointment in Nina's face. There is always something disappointing about the sudden end of a journey of unknown length.

"You see," went on the Eminent Gentleman, "this lake is where the river starts from. There's a spring, so they tell me, at the bottom of it, coming from the hills up there."

"I see," said Nina.

"But even if you've reached the end of your journey," went on the Eminent Gentleman, "isn't there anything else I can show you? I've some flowers people say are well worth seeing. Or up at the house we might find some breakfast."

"We've had our breakfast," said Nina. "We cooked it ourselves over a fire. But—but it seems a dreadfully long time ago. And I'd love to see your flowers."

That was how Nina and Mr. Dawkins arrived back at the Other House in good time to make

themselves respectable for lunch—and how it
came about that they arrived in a big touring car
driven by a smart chauffeur, with a coat-of-arms
on the paneling and the boat and the sack of
stores on the floor at their feet. And Miss Lamb
was not at all cross, either. For one thing she could
see for herself that Nina was as happy and as
healthy as she could be, and that she certainly had
not caught cold in the dreadful night air. For another thing she had implicit trust in Mr. Dawkins.
For another—she was resolute in keeping herself
as modern as she could be, and she knew that modern ideas were favorable to even little girls running wild occasionally. And she could see something, too, in both Dawkins' and Nina's faces
which had not been there before they went off on
this wild excursion—something of new kindliness
and fellowship; and it was not lost on her that
Nina was calling Dawkins "daddy." The fact that
they had breakfasted in the house of the Eminent
Gentleman (whose name meant much more to her
than to Dawkins) and had come home in his car
was the crowning argument in their favor. Miss
Lamb sat at lunch and listened to Nina's excited
account of the voyage, from the narrow escape

from shipwreck on a cow to their final reception on the lake. Miss Lamb did not realize that this first primitive excursion would lead in the end to the three of them making trips along rivers in the most unheard-of places—that her next sight of Paris would be from Mr. Dawkins' cabin motor-cruiser on the Seine.

CHAPTER XVII

IT WAS only a few days after this, one Friday afternoon, that Mary the parlor-maid brought in to Dawkins in his study a letter on a tray.

"A boy's just brought this on a bicycle, sir," she said. "He said it was urgent."

Mr. Dawkins opened it and read:

> "Gilding High School for Girls,
> "Gilding,
> "Surrey.

"Dear Sir:

"I regret to have to inform you that your ward Nina this afternoon has been guilty of very bad conduct, including malicious damage to property, avoidance of lessons, rudeness to mistresses, and finally inciting her fellow pupils to similar offenses. There is no need to remind you, I am sure, of the seriousness of all these actions, for each of which she is liable to expulsion from the school. I sincerely hope, however, that I shall not have to resort to such an extreme measure, and I trust that you will be able to show Nina her conduct in its true light, as at the moment of writing she is still inclined to treat the matter with a levity which I can only describe as most unpleasant.

"I am retaining her at school for an extra half-hour to make sure that my messenger will deliver this letter to you before her arrival home, in order that you will be able to make your plans for convincing her of the impropriety of her conduct, so that she will be able on Monday to say she is sorry.

"Yours truly,

"Edith M. Willow,

"Headmistress."

Mr. Dawkins read this letter and read it again. He even turned it over and looked at its blank back in search of further enlightenment. He was appalled by Miss Willow's horrible catalogue of Nina's crimes, and he had a sinking feeling at his heart until he brought himself to realize that what Miss Willow meant by her academic "impropriety of conduct" was not what some people would have meant. Nina had clearly been a very naughty girl, and it was up to him to make her sorry for it, since apparently Miss Willow had been unsuccessful. What on earth did one do to naughty girls? If Nina had been a boy he would not have had to think twice about that—but then neither would the authorities. With a girl it was different. He couldn't spank Nina. And anyway, he would have to find out what on earth it was she had done. He read Miss Willow's list again and felt no wiser. He thought for a moment of consulting Miss Lamb, but he put the idea aside. This was his job. He was still in a condition of confused debate when he heard the front door open to Nina, and he was about to ring and ask for her when the study door opened and Nina looked round it. Their eyes met, and Nina came in, noting the letter which Dawkins was twisting nervously in his fingers. But she did not seem at all frightened.

"Now what in the name of fortune," began Dawkins sternly, "have you been up to? Miss Willow has written saying you ought to be expelled from school."

"She told me she was writing to you," said Nina.

"And what did you say to that?"

"I said—I said I didn't think it would do much good."

That was a facer for a start, but Dawkins was not deterred.

"I'm not angry yet," he said, "because I don't know what it is you've done. You must tell me that first."

Dawkins prided himself that he had caught exactly the right tone of pained justice and conveyed the right suggestion of inexorable punishment. Nina quite admired him for it, but then Nina really looked for things to admire about Dawkins.

"It wasn't very much," she said. "Really it wasn't, except that I started laughing and couldn't stop myself, and that made Miss Willow wild and Miss Shorter wild."

"Begin at the beginning," said Dawkins solemnly.

"I've told you about the beginning already," said Nina. "I told you last week. You know, about how IIIB were always making fun of IIIA and calling us names and upsetting our desks when they got the chance. It's been going on for—oh, for years and years now."

"And what did you do about it?"

"Oh, some of us wanted to do one thing and some of us something else, at first. But all silly things, you know, like sending them a note saying what we thought about them. That wouldn't have been any good at all, so I—so we made up our minds to do something worth doing. Before prayers this morning Jean Mason sneaked into the hall and put a whole lot of Seccotine on their bench— at least she meant it to be their bench but it wasn't theirs at all because she was in such a hurry, it was IVB's, and when they stood up to say prayers when Miss Willow came in the bench came up with them and fell down with a bang just when Miss Willow was beginning 'dearly beloved.' And IVB guessed it was us and were simply *furious,* and IIIB went on like anything about it and so we *had* to do something."

"M'm," said Mr. Dawkins.

"You see on Friday afternoons we have singing for all the Thirds together in the hall, that's when Mr. Newton comes, and we stay there for two periods straight off. So we made up our minds about it in the dinner hour, and after dinner Betty Slaughter and I hooked off and hid in the cloak-rooms while the others went in to singing, because we knew we shouldn't be missed by old Mr. Newton. And we had our needles and cotton with us and

when singing started we went to IIIB's hooks and
we took their coats and we began to sew up all
their sleeves—with little tiny stitches so that they
wouldn't be able to undo them easily. And we
sewed up all the sleeves, and Betty started doing
some of 'em twice, and I tied all the shoelaces together in big hard knots and started sewing up the
boot bags. And when we'd nearly sewed 'em all
up we heard some people coming in from the garden, and when I peeped out of the window it was
IVB coming in from practical botany and Miss
Shorter was with them and we didn't know what
to do.

"So we hid in one of the boot holes—we just
managed to climb up and squeeze in and the coats
hung over us and I got hold of an attaché case and
stood it up in front of our legs and we stood there,
and IVB came in with Miss Shorter and they had to
change their shoes and they took hours. And Miss
Shorter kept on saying, 'Hurry up, girls.' And every time she said it we wanted to laugh and we
held on to each other and tried ever so hard not to
laugh. It was awful because Betty got the hiccups
and every now and then she'd give a tremendous
great 'Hic!' that made us want to laugh all the

more. Miss Shorter heard one of the 'hics' and said, 'Whatever's that?' because she was standing just by us and it wasn't one of IVB. Betty said 'Hic' again, and Miss Shorter jumped, and we were simply bursting, and somehow the attaché case fell down with a terrific bang beside her and she jumped and she looked and Betty and I were shaking like anything trying not to laugh and then Miss Shorter said, 'Why, there are some girls in the boot hole!' Just as she said it Betty went 'Hic!' again louder than ever, and we fell out of the boot hole and Miss Shorter screamed. We started laughing then, and laughed and laughed, and Miss Shorter was trying to ask us what we were doing there, and we couldn't stop so that she got crosser and crosser. And IVB started laughing too and Miss Shorter said, 'I will not have this impertinence,' and stamped her foot. Betty hiccuped again, awfully loud, and we all laughed, that time.

"And then Miss Shorter said, 'If you two girls do not try to behave yourselves *at once* I shall take you straight to Miss Willow.' But Betty went on hiccuping and so we went on laughing, IVB and all.

"And Miss Shorter was terribly angry and all

red in the face and she stood IVB up in line against the wall and told them not to move, not if anything happened at all. She said, 'You come with me,' to us, and she took us up-stairs, and we had to keep on stopping to laugh so that she got raving mad. We marched into Miss Willow's room and Miss Shorter tried to tell Miss Willow about how she found us in the cloak-room trying to dodge lessons and how rude we had been to her.

"Miss Willow looked very angry and said, 'What have you got to say about this?' to us. We might have said something, but just then we heard the Thirds come out of the hall and we knew they were going down to the cloak-room and so IIIB would find out about their coats and things, and Betty caught my eye and we laughed so hard I broke my elastic and of course that made Betty laugh all the more, and it made Miss Willow most fearfully cross. She said, 'I will stand you up with your faces to the wall until you recover yourselves!'

"Oh, and Miss Howe—that's the nice fat one, you know—had come in and she said, 'Hadn't I better get the poor child a safety pin first?' That made us shriek all over again.

"We simply didn't know what to do, and when we had nearly got over that I thought of IVB still standing against the wall in the cloak-room downstairs and that started it again. Miss Willow was standing up at her desk looking perfectly *awful*, and she was just going to say something more when in came Miss Mackie of IIIB and she was angry too, and Betty just shrieked with laughing and fell into my arms and we sat down on the floor because we couldn't stand up any longer.

"Miss Mackie said, 'Some one has been behaving *dreadfully* down in the cloak-room,' and Miss Willow said, 'Indeed?' and Miss Mackie told her that all her girls had found their coats sewn up and their boot bags sewn up and they were having to unpick them and there weren't *nearly* enough scissors to go round and IIIA was being very naughty. Oh, and she told Miss Shorter that she'd found IVB standing against the wall and they were still there and wanted to go home and what was Miss Shorter going to do about it, and at every word she said Betty and I shrieked and I had such a pain with laughing and what with us laughing and Miss Mackie and Miss Shorter talking at each other and Miss Howe trying to put a safety pin into me Miss Willow was so worried she didn't know what to do.

"And other people came and knocked at the door and we could hear an *awful* noise coming up from the cloak-room underneath, and at last Miss Willow left Miss Howe with us and marched off with Miss Mackie and Miss Shorter down-stairs to put things right, so that Miss Howe was able to get the safety pin into me at last and we managed to stop laughing and Miss Howe brushed us down and told us how naughty we were, but we knew that Miss Howe likes us to be naughty. And—and—that's all that happened except that when Miss Willow came back she tried to be angry with us and she shut me into one room and Betty into another while she wrote to Betty's mother and you, but I had Miss Howe with me and it didn't matter. Miss Mackie was in with Betty and I can't *think* what she said to her because Miss Mackie is an awful cat just like all the other IIIB's. And after Miss Willow had written the letters she had us back in her study to lecture us about how wicked we had been, but I had such a pain from laughing that I couldn't listen to what she was saying, and when she asked me to repeat

what she had said I told her so. If it hadn't been
for Miss Howe I don't know what she would have
done, but Miss Howe quieted her down—she
is a brick, you know. And then she let us go and
Miss Howe put me into the bus to come home."

"M'm," said Dawkins. Words can hardly ex-
press the extent of his relief. "You know it *was*
very naughty of you, don't you?"

"Y—yes," said Nina.

Dawkins racked his brains for something else to
say, but the words did not come too easily, especially as he had a feeling that incidents of this
kind constituted the better part of "education" in
its wide sense. "I hope you will tell Miss Willow
that you are sorry, on Monday." Dawkins felt the
inadequacy of this even as he said it.

"I don't think I *am* sorry," said Nina.

And then Dawkins saw an avenue of approach,
and took it desperately.

"But it was very rude of you to laugh when
Miss Willow and Miss—er—Shorter were talking
to you," he said. "It's worse than yawning and all
the other things Miss Lamb tells you about. It's
very rude."

"Um. Yes. I hadn't thought of that," said Nina.

"Well, that's what you had better apologize about. Go up to Miss Willow and Miss Shorter and say you're sorry you were so rude to them."

It is doubtful whether even this line of argument would have been very convincing to Nina if she had not caught the gleam in Dawkins' eye. There was a sort of twinkle there—it was the winking of the augur. Nina grinned at Dawkins, and Dawkins grinned back helplessly.

"Righto," said Nina. "That's what I'll do. Oh, and I *do* want some tea."

And that was all Dawkins could manage in the way of correction in the matter. He could not see anything evil in Nina's behavior on that occasion, and it was more than he could manage to simulate indignation—with Nina looking at him with the eyes of the Hawk, that is to say. Nevertheless he felt justified in writing to Miss Willow that he had spoken very seriously indeed to Nina on the subject of her behavior and that he hoped he had brought her to reason, as her apologies would prove. But even as he wrote his mouth twisted as he drew a mental comparison between his present activities and those of a year ago. He preferred the present ones.

CHAPTER XVIII

BETTY SLAUGHTER was a plump and jolly little girl, so plump indeed that the sight of her rounded contours had made Miss Willow's palm itch during that deplorable interview in her room. She and Nina were bosom friends, and no one, noting, as Dawkins did, her solidity both mental and physical, could have any doubt at all about who had taken the initiative in the campaign of reprisals against IIIB.

Betty was the only child of her mother who was a widow; and Mrs. Gateson-Slaughter (Betty had to put up with an abbreviated surname owing to the school rule against hyphens) was a fairly well-known figure in the second circle of Gilding society. We may take it for granted that she had already heard from her daughter about her friend Nina Royle and had not taken much notice. But later, just before the grand catastrophe described in the last chapter, she had found that Nina Royle was the ward of Mr. Dawkins, and her interest increased enormously. For prominent in Mrs. Gateson-Slaughter's set were the manager and the first cashier of the Gilding branch of the National County Bank, and both these gentlemen were married and not entirely discreet—and they were exceedingly interested in Mr. Henry Dawkins of the Other House.

For several months now Mr. Dawkins had entered the Gilding branch at fairly regular intervals of a few weeks, and had paid in large sums of money—anything between five thousand and twenty thousand pounds at a time, mainly in checks but partly in three months' bills which he had discounted. Nearly all this money Mr. Dawkins had invested in gilt-edged securities of a range which excited the manager's respect; he owned British Government stock and Corporation loans and Dominion stock, Egyptian and Soudanese loans, and few of the really secure securities such as bank shares and brewing debentures. So far the stream of investment showed no signs of coming to an end, and the manager and the cashier had ceased to expect an end and had begun to look upon Mr. Dawkins as a man with an income averaging ten thousand pounds a month—which was a very considerable income even for Gilding, round which clustered the sub-suburban palaces of a score of millionaires. The general ignorance about Mr. Dawkins excited gossip, and gossip had little enough to go on. But it sufficed that Mrs. Gateson-Slaughter should know that Mr. Dawkins was reputed to be immensely rich and that his ward should be a friend of her daughter. Miss Willow's letter to her regarding Betty's deplorable conduct arrived at the psychological moment. Mrs. Gateson-Slaughter girded up her loins and set out on the campaign which she sketched out to herself brilliantly, and which was devised to end a troublous widowhood on a despicably small pension.

Mr. Dawkins was quite pleasantly surprised one afternoon at the Other House when Mary the maid brought in a card inscribed "Mrs. Gateson-Slaughter." He had the lady brought in to the drawing-room, and nervously ordered tea, feeling heartily uncomfortable that Miss Lamb should have gone shopping in Gilding. He did not know that Mrs. Gateson-Slaughter had made sure of this by actual observation before she called.

One glimpse of Mrs. Gateson-Slaughter revealed the origin of that comfortable plumpness on Betty's part which has already been remarked. For Mrs. Gateson-Slaughter, if she could hardly be called fat, was at least substantially covered. But she was over average height, and well gowned and hatted—and corseted, for that expression regarding the girding of her loins was by no means figurative. She made a fine figure of a woman in consequence as she came forward to Mr. Dawkins and tendered him a small plump hand in an elegant glove.

"I hope you won't think too badly of me, Mr. Dawkins," she said, "for calling on you in this fashion, but I felt I simply had to come and talk over with you this very unfortunate business at the school, about your ward and my daughter, you know."

"Oh—er—yes, of course," said Mr. Dawkins, at last forming a mental connection between Betty Slaughter and this magnificent Mrs. Gateson-Slaughter. "Won't you sit down?"

Mrs. Gateson-Slaughter sat down and looked about her while the maid brought in tea. The house was small, of course, but not too small. It was furnished quite expensively in very good taste; there were signs of a fair-sized domestic staff; the gardens, as far as her lightning glance before entering the house could tell, were well kept, and Mrs. Gateson-Slaughter well knew what a sure indication of the financial barometer this was; and she had seen a gardener and a boy at work in them. She also knew the make and price of Mr. Dawkins' car. Altogether she deduced, very soundly, that there must be plenty of money in the establishment, although she had to admit that if rumor spoke truly regarding his wealth Mr. Dawkins was not spending one twentieth of his income. However, she was satisfied that she would have no cause to regret it if her pension were to lapse on her remarriage.

"Won't you have some tea?" asked Mr. Dawkins.

"Thank you."

"And—er—hadn't you better pour out?"

"Of course, if you like."

Mrs. Gateson-Slaughter busied herself very efficiently with the tea things.

"Milk? Sugar? Thank you, I will have some toast."

Mrs. Gateson-Slaughter had very white plump hands (oh, the care she lavished on them every day) with pink finger-nails like daggers. They were rather fascinating hands, and their owner displayed them to the best advantage. In fact, Dawkins' attention was riveted so closely upon them that he had to recall himself with a jerk.

"It was a very bad shock for me, Mr. Dawkins," she said, "when that letter arrived saying that Betty was liable to expulsion. I suppose Miss Willow wrote to you in the same way? I was most unhappy at the thought of my daughter's future being jeopardized like that, until she came home and told what had really happened. But Betty was full of admiration for your Nina, Mr. Dawkins."

This last sentence was the first of a well-planned series. Mrs. Gateson-Slaughter wanted to find out all Mr. Dawkins' soft spots as quickly as possible. She could not properly appreciate the state of mind of a grown man who could be deeply interested about an eleven-year-old girl, but of course it was possible. And Mr. Dawkins' pleased smile and nervous movement told her that it was true enough, and that one way to his heart was a proper interest in Nina. She resolved to play for safety and keep to the topic until further developments occurred spontaneously.

"Of course," she said, "I expect Betty was just as responsible for what happened as Nina was. It's very difficult, isn't it, to get to the bottom of children's naughtiness? I tried for a long time to get out of Betty why she did all that, but she wouldn't say anything except that she and Nina 'thought they would.' "

"It was some kind of a feud, I believe," said Dawkins, in the careful accent he was learning from Miss Lamb, "between their form and some other form."

"Oh, yes," said Mrs. Gateson-Slaughter, "I found out in the end that something like that was the matter"—actually she had made no attempt at all, not being interested in Betty's behavior—"but I should like to know why it was our two girls who had to do it, and not any of the others."

It was beyond Dawkins' will or capacity to explain that the Hawk's daughter could hardly help taking the lead in a feud. But he had a curiously grateful feeling about the "our" which Mrs. Gateson-Slaughter had deliberately employed. It almost elevated him to respectable parenthood.

"These things are very much a matter of chance, I suppose," he said.

"Yes, I suppose so. But it would have been dreadful if Miss Willow had really expelled Betty. I can't think what I should have done. Children are a great worry, Mr. Dawkins, don't you think so? Or haven't you had enough experience to judge?"

"No—er—I'm not married."

That was just what Mrs. Gateson-Slaughter had wanted to make sure about.

"It was very brave of you, then, to look after Nina like this. She was the daughter of a relation, I suppose?"

"No, of a very great friend of mine who died."

"How sad! And does Nina resemble her very much?"

"Oh, I only knew her father—he was the friend I spoke about."

Mrs. Gateson-Slaughter added to her mental dossier that Nina, at any rate, was not connected directly or indirectly with any affair of Mr. Dawkins' heart—she realized that her most formidable rival to the affection of this bachelor of nearly forty would be a sentimental recollection. Her hopes and her spirits were rising every moment.

She led the conversation dexterously this way

and that, exploring tentatively all Dawkins' tastes and tendencies and found them peculiarly unsatisfactory. He had no soul for art or literature or music, seemingly. He did not hunt—that she knew already. He played golf, but Mrs. Gateson-Slaughter, looking keenly at him under lowered eyelids in the way she had, could not detect any glow of enthusiasm for the game. He did not play bridge, and that was a pity, for Mrs. Gateson-Slaughter was the best player in Gilding, and her winnings paid her laundry bills. Apparently he did some work, but his remarks about it were vague and unsatisfactory, beyond the information conveyed that it took up only half his time—she could not, of course, be expected to realize that his remarks were so vague because he was rather shy about owning to an interest in charitable work. Search whichever way she would, she could not find any enthusiasms anywhere in the man save for the hardly credible one about Nina. That gave her a better measure of the task before her; it is far more difficult to entrap a man who has no enthusiasms to run away with him.

Mrs. Gateson-Slaughter was about to take her departure to give herself an opportunity to digest the data she had collected when they heard fresh arrivals at the door. They were Nina and Miss Lamb, come home on the afternoon bus, the one from school and the other from shopping. Mrs. Gateson-Slaughter smiled sweetly at them as Dawkins awkwardly made the introductions. She eyed Miss Lamb straightly, for in her, at first, she sensed a possible rival, or at least an enemy. But one glance at the thick spectacles, at the trace of gray just appearing in her hair, at the untouched-up lips and hardly-powdered cheeks, at the flat bosom and unassertive manner satisfied her, and she dropped Miss Lamb contemptuously out of mind. But Nina was different. She stood at Miss Lamb's side, both of them rather wordless in consequence of the surprise of finding an elegant lady visitor in the drawing-room. Nina's clean palate detected through her dilated nostrils an unaccustomed scent in the room, a very feminine, elegant scent which Nina instantly decided to dislike for the rest of her life. She decided, too, instinctively that she disliked Mrs. Gateson-Slaughter's plump, well-corseted figure, and her well-massaged cheeks, and her pretty hands with their cruel nails. In fact there was nothing about Mrs. Gateson-Slaughter of which Nina even faintly approved. And all because of the friendly, familiar attitudes of Dawkins and Mrs. Gateson-Slaughter on either side of the tea-table as she entered the room.

Mrs. Gateson-Slaughter, on the other hand, did not bother her mind about whether she liked Nina or not. She paid no attention to the long chin and the steady gray eyes. All she wanted to do was to receive Nina in a fashion which would please Dawkins. She made the attempt prettily enough.

"So this is Nina," she said, both hands out, with a pretty modulation of her contralto voice, "I've heard such a lot about you from Betty. I'm Betty's mother."

Nina reluctantly gave her one hand and suffered herself to be drawn effusively into range and pecked upon the cheek.

"Of course, you and Betty are great friends," said Mrs. Gateson-Slaughter. "You must come and see us quite soon."

As she spoke she half-included, by her gesture, Mr. Dawkins, but not Miss Lamb, who was accustomed, of course, to similar omissions.

"Thank you," said Nina soberly, apparently not overwhelmed by the prospect.

"And now," said Mrs. Gateson-Slaughter, "I must run off. Good-by, Miss er—er. Good-by, Nina, dear. Good-by, Mr. Dawkins. Our little talk has quite put new hope into me. Thank you *so* much. Oh, please don't bother——"

Her voice died away down the hall as Mr. Dawkins overrode her half-hearted protests and escorted her to the door. Miss Lamb and Nina looked at each other. They heard the conversation at the door bubble up again momentarily, and they heard Mr. Dawkins come back for his hat. Then they heard the purr of the motor-car engine being started, and the sound of the wheels on the gravel. Mr. Dawkins had not been so churlish as not to offer his caller a lift back into the town. Miss Lamb sought to keep her features expressionless as she rang the bell for more tea, but she was unsuccessful. Nina was much too acute for her.

CHAPTER XIX

MRS. GATESON-SLAUGHTER had no wish to rush matters. She said little to Mr. Dawkins while at his side in the car, and she stopped him and got out on the very outskirts of Gilding, on the plea that she had other calls to make. She contented herself with a brilliant opening of her dark eyes as she said good-by to him on the pavement. Then she hastened away, leaving Dawkins to stare after her for a second or two before climbing back into the car.

He was by no means a bad-looking man, she said to herself as she walked away. She always liked blue eyes, and even if his hair wasn't golden there was a lot of life and light in it. His manner was rather brusk and shy, but that wouldn't matter much, and he had obviously a nice quiet taste in good clothes. As far as outward appearance went he would be a highly satisfactory husband; those burly shoulders of his and his towering figure would attract attention wherever they went. He had money enough, too, seemingly. And clearly he was a bit of a fool, which would be an advantage. But he was not a bit foolish, for all that. She would have to be very careful. No use pretending she was much younger than she actually was—with a twelve-year-old daughter to give her the lie. He could do simple addition as well as the next man. She would have to own to thirty-two at least. And on second thoughts she would own to her full age of thirty-five. That was a sacrifice, seeing that she did not look a day more than a full-bosomed twenty-nine. But it was a sacrifice well worth making, for he was the sort of man to whom honesty and frankness would appeal—and to whom thirty-five would appeal too. That just showed what a clever woman Mrs. Gateson-Slaughter was. She let herself into her little house in a side street off Gilding High Street with her latch-key. Betty was there, and she looked up eagerly from her home work at the sound of the key and ran to greet her. But Mrs. Gateson-Slaughter put her aside.

"Oh, don't bother me, please," she said. "You know I don't like fussing about."

Mr. Dawkins drove back in a curiously disturbed state of mind. It was the first time in all his life that he had been in equal social contact with a woman of Mrs. Gateson-Slaughter's apparent class. He had not as yet even had much to do with the semidowdy lady members of the golf club. This superb woman of the splendid eyes and assured bearing, humanized by motherly love, was something different. He could jest with and be beloved by the slatternly, too-fecund mothers of the settlement; he could associate without awkwardness, but with an unconscious shy courtesy which left memories laden with regrets, with the hardened women of the streets who had shared his reckless moments, but he realized that normally he would be very discomposed by contact with a lady who knew she was a lady. But he had been perfectly at ease with Mrs. Gateson-Slaughter directly after the first plunge. And those exquisite hands of hers! Mr. Dawkins knew men's hands, and chapped coarsened hands, and Nina's brown paws, and Miss Lamb's unobtrusive thin hands, although he had never paid much attention to these last. But he had never known hands like Mrs. Gateson-Slaughter's before—so knowledgable and cared-for, worldly-wise sort of hands, masterful hands and yet completely feminine. And that faint suspicion of fulness about her hips and throat—that tiniest hint of fleshiness! It brought a whole train of rose-colored thoughts, quite formless, into Mr. Dawkins' mind. They surged through his brain so suddenly that he had to take a grip on himself with a start and lighten the pressure on the accelerator pedal. That kind of thought was hardly compatible with driving along a main road. He came carefully back to the Other House.

Let no one ever try to guess what a child is thinking or is likely to think. Nina at eleven was a bundle of intuitions and instincts and lightning deductions. Never before had the possibility occurred to her of Dawkins being attracted to a woman, still less of his marrying one. The sublime egotism of childhood had taken it for granted that his life would be henceforth devoted to her service, but that afternoon it suffered a terrible shock. Nina had known the tender mercies of a step-grandmother; she had no wish to encounter those of a step-guardian. Personal fear was blended with personal jealousy. She wanted Dawkins all to herself. And, besides, Mrs. Gateson-Slaughter had a very decided personality, one which made itself felt immediately in the close confines of the drawing-room (very possibly Nina, child-fashion, was confusing scent and personality), and Nina had all the personality one room could hold. For her to meet another was like the drawing together of two opposite-charged thunder-clouds.

Nina, at tea, took note, with childish cunning, of Miss Lamb's silence, and drew deductions from it at the same time as she forbore to comment. For Miss Lamb had much the same feelings as Nina. At the moment she had all that heart could desire, a house to manage, a man's wants to anticipate, a child to cherish. But a lifetime of migration had impressed upon her the fleetingness of the good things of this world. Were Mr. Dawkins to marry, as she suddenly realized was possible, and were his wife to find no use for her or to take a dislike to Nina's presence in the house and send her to a boarding-school, and all these were possible, too, then Miss Lamb would be cast out into an unloving world to begin again the dreary round of governessing or schoolmistressing. And in the very distant gray future (Miss Lamb mentally put her hands tremulously over her eyes and shunned the prospect, but she knew it was there) lay only the horrible dreariness of a home for decayed gentle-

women. Miss Lamb was sore afraid. So the two of
them were very quiet during tea-time, and Dawkins, returning, was uncomfortably conscious of a
state of strain in the atmosphere of the drawing-
room, and of a reproachful look in Nina's eyes as
she glanced up at his entrance. But Dawkins, the
thick-headed dolt, could not guess the reason.

During the days that followed the fear which
had grown suddenly into the lives of Nina and
Miss Lamb sank below the surface; it was not
obvious, but it was always there, deep down. But
the beauties of the surface were undeniable, and
kept it hidden. That craze of Dawkins and Nina
about running water blossomed out to the most
amazing extent. The little green collapsible boat
was good enough for little tentative excursions on
the garden river, but it hardly fell in with their
expanding ideas. One or two mysterious journeys
by Mr. Dawkins to Thames-side boat-houses resulted one day in his carrying off Nina and Miss
Lamb to Windsor and displaying to them a real
motor-boat, a cabin cruiser with two berths in the
cabin and a well in which people could sleep in
addition, with a tiny pantry and galley, a most
exquisite affair altogether. Nina went into raptures

about it straightway, and did not even demand to be taken for a cruise on the spot, so busy was she prying into lockers and touching the shiny brass-work and the primus stoves and the handy canteen in the galley.

Even Miss Lamb caught the infection and was impressed by the cunning with which space was saved and the household convenience considered. And the bright solid paintwork and varnish were a joy to her; she did not blench when Nina and Daw-kins together announced that very shortly—when the summer holidays came, in fact—the boat would be her home for days together.

This last decision had been reached by Dawkins in fumbling fashion. He did not understand his motives, and he did not try to, either. But there was an awkwardness about living in cramped quar-ters alone with Nina, child though she was. He looked to Miss Lamb to help him out of the diffi-culty; besides, there was no question of his inhabit-ing the little cabin with its five feet of headroom in the center; motor-boat cabins are not designed for men of his inches. And it is just possible that he looked ahead to an ill-defined future when Nina would be a child no longer and cruising *à deux* would be unthinkable to his sober mind—even if, as was highly probable, no thought of such difficulty ever occurred to Nina.

So Nina's summer holiday was spent by the three of them exploring the Thames, the most modest of rivers which only displays her full beauties to the sincerely devout among her lovers. The *Baby* (that was the only name Dawkins' unimaginative mind could devise after they had agreed that "Nina" untranslated would be inconvenient) nosed her way up-stream at first, past the glories of Cliveden and Marlow and Wargrave, past the ugliness of Reading and all the sweet beauty of Mapledurham and Cleve to the twin hills of Wittenham, until they reached that most definite of goals, Folly Bridge at Oxford. They went slowly enough, calling the aid of the dingey to explore the backwaters which were too weedy or shallow to accommodate the big boat.

And everybody blossomed out most amazingly. Miss Lamb's elegant face and ladylike nose were burned to a fiery red by the sun on the water, and her skin came off in flakes, but she didn't mind a bit. The careless life found her without a care. It was all so natural that Nina and Dawkins did not find it at all surprising to see Miss Lamb with her skirt kilted above her knees, splashing about in a backwater helping the dingey over summer shallows. She produced a most amazing sunbonnet which gave her an old-fashioned appearance which contrasted with her modern clothes as satisfactorily as mustard with beef so that she looked completely adorable. Her one failing was her childish fear of the primus stoves and their suspected propensity for blowing up the unwary, and this, as it happened, was of no importance; for Dawkins revealed himself in a new light as a cook of the first order. He prepared most delightful meals for them; they indulged in wild orgies of steak and onions, and he had a very deft hand for omelettes, so that Miss Lamb's usually birdlike appetite expanded until she could hold her own even with Nina. And she showed no signs of thinking it out of place that at nightfall Dawkins should come into the cabin to kiss Nina good night while she was in bed as well in the opposite berth, in her severe night-gown with her hair plaited. The magic of running water had affected her, too.

Altogether they explored the Thames very thoroughly indeed, that summer. They made a mighty

trip down the upper river from Lechlade in a skiff,
leaving the *Baby* at Oxford, and spending a couple
of nights in hotels. They paddled the dingey up
St. Patrick's stream and the Loddon and the Thame
and the half-hundred other wonderful little rivers
which contribute to the magic of the Thames. In
fact, time flew so rapidly that Dawkins' calcula-
tions were brought to nought. He had planned to
visit the Lower Thames, too, to take the *Baby*
down past the bridges and the Pool out to the
Nore, but September only found them heading
back for Windsor. They did not regret what they
had missed; it had all been too lovely, from the
lazy days of idle cruising up-stream, and the long
adventurous voyages in the dingey, to the morning shopping excursions in little, sleepy, sun-
steeped villages and the vast meals and the wonderful entrancing evenings when the Thames looks
her loveliest and stillness creeps out over the water.

There had been all the delights of swimming,
too. Dawkins swam with the skill and power to
be expected of a man of his bulk, but when they
first started out Nina not only could not swim but
was slightly scared at being expected to try. That
feeling soon passed, however, when Dawkins

found a bit of river three feet deep with a gravelly bottom and stood there in the sunshine in all the tremendous splendor of his muscular symmetry and invited her to join him. From rather timid splashings Nina passed in a few days to complete confidence, and soon with her hands on Dawkins' shoulders would allow him to swim with her wherever he liked, although it seemed as if she would never, never be able to swim by herself and remember to breathe in only when her mouth and nose were above water. Then all at once toward the end of the holidays she suddenly found that she could, and swam a whole twenty yards toward Dawkins before it dawned upon her what she was doing and she started splashing again. Next time she swam properly, in her glaring little red costume, and by the time they came home she was already beginning to imitate Dawkins' powerful overarm stroke, even though in her heart of hearts she feared she would never be able to copy the clean vigorous manner in which he dived from the counter of the *Baby*. And she was thoroughly sunburned and happy, and her thin face had freckled so much that with her pointed chin it looked exactly like a turkey's egg.

Not one of them, not even Miss Lamb, was pleased to come home to the Other House and civilization and school again, but through the dark and hopeless winter they found a way of cheering themselves up, and that was with maps and imagination. Maps had played a great part in their river tour, and even Nina had learned to read them properly and place where they were and what was the nearest way to shops and water. When, during that winter, they felt the old urge coming over them they found that the surest way toward relief was to spread the maps before them and remember past adventures and plan fresh ones.

Miss Lamb discovered a new outlet for her tiny little talent for drawing, so far employed only in her feeble little water-colors and sketches. In the privacy of her own room, with copies of very old charts for models, she spent a good many happy hours before she proudly displayed to Nina and Dawkins the first half of the Chart of the Cruise of the *Baby*. This was a most wonderful affair—a long, long strip of paper bearing a pictorial history of the cruise. Miss Lamb had lavished detail upon it with the same loving kindness with which she lavished attention upon Dawkins and Nina.

Right from the beginning with its legend, "Here Ys Windsore," every detail of the cruise was displayed in little drawings beside the windings of the river in the plan. "Here be Mermaydes" showed Nina swimming valiantly. "Here they doe offer up burnt Sacrifices" showed the mouth of the Thames and some one faintly recognizable as Dawkins dancing round a pyre—a little reminder of the time when Dawkins, summoned from the galley by Nina in her excitement over some passing herons, forgot that he had left the sausages in the frying-pan. Nina and Dawkins fell in love with it on the spot, and it was pinned in its appointed place as a dado round Nina's play-room and added to strip by strip as time went on. Nina often told herself proudly that no girl in England had such a fine dado to look at. There was always something new to find in it; for it was Miss Lamb's one masterpiece on a heroic scale—that one mightiest achievement which every one of us is capable of attaining once in our lives. It was the fair blossom called forth by the sun of happiness which of late had so warmed Miss Lamb's spinsterly being. And Nina's and Dawkins' enthusiastic praises called forth the prettiest blushes to her fading cheeks.

Future ambitions blended with past memories. Nina roamed over the map of Europe seeking fresh worlds to conquer. Dawkins and she debated solemnly about the Seine and the Loire and the Rhine and the Danube. Nina caught her breath with excitement at the thought of penetrating past Vienna and Budapest even to the Black Sea. They compromised by deciding next summer merely on a vast tour through France—Dawkins with great diligence and by the aid of innumerable maps and text-books succeeded in discovering that it was possible to travel nearly two thousand kilometers by water in France without retracing one's steps. There came a time when a casual remark from Dawkins enlightened Nina to the fact that the river system of the Amazon, seemingly, from the map, so well defined and clear-cut, was in reality half unknown, and that there were hundreds and hundreds of miles of broad tributaries as yet untraveled by white men. The conversation ended by their solemnly swearing to travel those rivers together, mapping and exploring, as soon as ever Nina was grown up. Nina meant every word of her vow when she made it, looking excitedly into Dawkins' eyes; so did Dawkins.

CHAPTER XX

BUT that winter there were many other things to think about besides plans and projects. Nina was in IV-A now at school, and Dawkins was having to remember his entirely forgotten Latin in order to help with her home work. And Betty Slaughter had moved up to IVA too.

That was the trouble. For Betty, besides having a splendid admiration for Nina, would also frequently convey her invitations to visit her mother. Nina was fond enough of Betty—she was a splendid half-back at hockey who played up to Nina on the wing in true comradely style—but she hated those visits to Mrs. Gateson-Slaughter's, hard though she would have found it to explain her dislike. Betty was the soul of chattering hospitality and her mother at the tea-table unbent to her most graciously. It was, it is to be supposed, that unbending which annoyed Nina. It did not ring quite true. Although it is hardly likely that Nina

pieced together the evidence and drew logical
conclusions from it in adult fashion, she nevertheless perceived Mrs. Gateson-Slaughter's offhanded-
ness toward Betty, and she sensed her entire lack of
interest in children, and she was consequently suspicious of the lady's ostentatious kindness toward
her, flinching instinctively away from it. Let Mrs.
Gateson-Slaughter spread her snares ever so subtly,
Nina always contrived to avoid them while ignoring them, thereby nettling the lady considerably.
There were queer moments at tea-time when sparks
seemed on the point of flying; when Nina and Mrs.
Gateson-Slaughter grew suddenly formal toward
each other and oddly stiff in their manner—"bri-
dling" would be an exaggerated way of describing
it, but even Betty was puzzled and hurt at this
vague friction.

These visits of Nina's, however, undoubtedly
served their purpose to Mrs. Gateson-Slaughter's
mind. For sometimes it was Mr. Dawkins who
came in the car to fetch her home, and that meant
a few minutes' conversation with him while Nina
was putting on her hat and coat, and Mrs. Gateson-
Slaughter during those few minutes contrived to
be charmingly maternal and hospitable and lady-

like and womanly, all at once, to the deep impressing of Dawkins. It was surprising how differently
Mrs. Gateson-Slaughter behaved when it was only
Miss Lamb who called for Nina—and on the occasions when Nina was to go home by herself Mrs.
Gateson-Slaughter verged even upon inhospitality
in her anxiety to speed the parting guest.

Then of course there were Betty's return visits,
which Betty enjoyed so thoroughly and pathetically that neither Miss Lamb nor Nina could raise
any objection to them. For well before it was time
for Betty to go home Mrs. Gateson-Slaughter
would arrive, tactfully attributing her earliness to
the irregularity of the bus service, and she would
talk away with Dawkins as hard as ever she could
—to say nothing of the trip home, when neither
Nina nor Miss Lamb would be present in the car
when Dawkins drove them into Gilding again.

Mrs. Gateson-Slaughter was playing an anxious
game with extreme skill. She knew she was fixed
in Gilding unless marriage unfixed her. The little
house was her own and all her friends lived in
Gilding, and her little income which enabled her
to move in nearly the best of Gilding society would
be nothing in London—it would only mean a

ghastly life in Balham or Gunnersbury, with far less chance of bettering her circumstances. The late Captain Slaughter (Gateson was her maiden name) had been before the war a professional man in the employ of the Gilding Urban District Council, and Mrs. Gateson-Slaughter just managed to make both ends meet by the aid of her officer's widow's pension, a tiny grant from the Council, an annuity purchased with the insurance money, and the government allowance for Betty's school fees.

She was popular enough in the local women's bridge club—if popularity could be said to exist among those greedy-fingered women—but, curiously, the very women who were willing to double her no-trumps were strangely backward when it came to encouraging her presence among their menfolk. The sons who went up to town on the eight thirty-three and returned on the five twenty were deftly headed off from her, rather to their bewilderment, and Mrs. Gateson-Slaughter (with one eye on the quite well-off Slaughter family and for her own marketability) had no use for the husbands. Since the war one or two wealthy bachelors without hampering female relatives had

sidled up to her and had sidled away again in
time, but none of them had been half as attractive
from any point of view as Mr. Dawkins. He was
wealthy, he was almost good-looking, and passable
enough in manners. He seemed a nice enough man
as far as she could tell in other directions—in fact,
it is to be believed that Mrs. Gateson-Slaughter
would have been really and genuinely in love with
him had not the spirit of calculation caught her
first. She was at any rate quite reconciled to the
possible adoption of the plebeian name of Dawkins in exchange for her own aristocratic hyphena-
tion.

In certain directions she found it hard to play
her part well. She could not enter into Dawkins'
and Nina's enthusiasm for ridiculous voyages under primitive conditions. She saved herself from
wrinkling a disgusted nose at their excited joint
account of orgies of steak and onions in the
cramped cabin of the *Baby,* and she tried to laugh
with them, but the laughter did not deceive Nina
at all and hardly deceived Dawkins. All that sort
of thing, she told herself grimly, would stop on
marriage—a yacht at Cowes or Monte Carlo if they
had to live on a boat, but nothing less. But for the

present she tried to imitate their enthusiasm—just as she tried to imitate Dawkins' enthusiasm for Nina. She played her cards with distinction, if not with brilliance.

Dawkins, meanwhile, was moving steadily into society. At the golf club, with his handicap down to nine, he was a really popular figure now that he was not so cautiously reserved. For one thing, he had gradually grown quite keen about the game, now that he had other interests and could not devote all his time to it, and that loosened his tongue a little. He had to buy himself evening clothes, the first he had ever possessed in his life, in which to attend the club dinners. He found himself being asked here and there occasionally, for an unattached and reputedly wealthy male is invaluable for making numbers even or replacing some one who had fallen out. Once or twice in return he gave, after consultation with Miss Lamb, little bachelor dinner parties at the Other House, beautifully cooked and served, thanks to Miss Lamb's anxious care, which helped him on the road to popularity. He received more than one assurance that if in the new year he chose to try again for membership in the Manor Club he would encounter no opposition. Things were developing quite placidly and normally when Mrs. Gateson-Slaughter decided to force the pace.

One December evening Nina had just got into bed. The light was still on and she lay for a moment listening to the torrential rain outside. This was the moment, settled by long custom, for Dawkins to make his appearance. Just as she had recovered from the shudderiness of the sheets he would come in in his friendly fashion with her hot milk and biscuits, and would reach himself a chair and sit down and listen while she chattered away to him in the intervals of milk and biscuits. When she had finished he would switch off the light and stoop over her in the dark, and she would put up her pajamaed arms to his neck for his good-night kiss, which, on her part, was usually milk-and-biscuity. That happened every evening on which Dawkins was free, which even now was at least four times a week, and it was a well-established part of the day's routine which sent Nina off to sleep quite happily.

But this evening it was not Dawkins who came into the little white bedroom, but his usual deputy, Miss Lamb.

"Oh," said Nina, disappointed, "isn't daddy coming in this evening?"

"No," said Miss Lamb, putting down milk and biscuits on the bedside table, "he's dining out."

"He didn't tell *me*," said Nina. "Did he wear his evening clothes? Where's he gone?"

There was no reason why Dawkins should not tell Nina, save that he felt awkward when Mrs. Gateson-Slaughter's name came up in conversation between them because, singularly, a little look of fear came into Nina's eyes on those occasions. And Mrs. Gateson-Slaughter had given the invitation so delicately—"Just a simple little dinner, so that we can talk, because there's such a lot I want to discuss with you about Betty and Nina, and we *do* get so interrupted if they're still up. And we're both old enough"—this with a friendly smile of common sense—"for people not to think anything of our dining *tête-à-tête*"—that he couldn't have got out of it if he had wanted to. But he had ridiculously flinched from telling Nina, although, to show there was nothing to hide, he had compromised by telling Miss Lamb his destination just before starting out. And Miss Lamb was so surprised that she could not help telling the truth to

Nina; and perhaps she was a little alarmed, too, and couldn't conceal that from Nina, either.

"He's dining at Mrs. Gateson-Slaughter's," said Miss Lamb. "Yes, he wore his evening clothes and he said he wouldn't be back very late."

"Oh," said Nina again.

Miss Lamb, as in duty bound, had loyally tried to keep her voice unconcerned, and had of course failed. For a second or two Nina and Miss Lamb were grown women as they eyed each other. But Miss Lamb knew her duty and her place.

"Come on, Nina. Drink up your milk so that I can turn your light out and you can go to sleep," she said.

Nina had no taste whatever now for milk or for biscuits, but with Miss Lamb's eye on her she acted as resolutely as ever her father had done against President Eguia. She ate her biscuits and drank her milk speedily and without a sign of distaste.

"Good night, dear," said Miss Lamb, with the faintest trace of a catch in her voice. They kissed each other in the darkness, and then Miss Lamb tiptoed out of the room.

Nina lay in bed with her thoughts revolving dizzily through her mind. She felt feverishly active.

She clenched her fists and her little teeth as she thought of Dawkins with Mrs. Gateson-Slaughter. There shot into her mind the memory of a recent conversation with Betty. The latter had let fall some unguarded expression on which Nina had seized instantly.

"What *do* you mean?" Nina had said.

"Oh, nothing, nothing at all," Betty had replied.

"You do mean something," pursued Nina relentlessly. "Come on, out with it."

Fat little Betty had tried to be stubborn, thin little Nina had been fiercely persistent.

"Oh, it's nothing really," yielded Betty at length, "it's just that—that mother said I must be nice to you and get Mr. Dawkins to like me in case—in case Mr. Dawkins and mother ever got married. That's all."

All? thought Nina to herself in bed. All? Her daddy marrying that woman! Nina knew positively and for certain that that would mean the end of all wild camping trips. They would never explore the Amazon together. And she wanted her daddy for herself, herself, herself. And there was a thread of unselfishness running through her thoughts, too, for she knew that her daddy would

not find permanent happiness, or any illusory likeness to it, in Mrs. Gateson-Slaughter's arms. With
all the fierce rapid decision to be expected of the
Hawk's daughter Nina threw off the bed-clothes
and swung her legs out of bed in the darkness.
She dared not switch on the light—Miss Lamb was
too watchful a guardian for her to risk a light
after lights out. She dressed in the dark, silently,
and then stood for a moment listening. She still
could hear nothing beside the noise of the rain
outside. She thought rapidly. Her macintosh and
greatcoat and rubber Wellingtons were down-stairs
in the cloak-room off the hall, and it would be use-
less to try to get hold of them with Miss Lamb in
the drawing-room next door. She would have to
go through the rain without them. For a moment
she debated the possibility of creeping down-stairs
and through the front door, but decided against it
for fear of encountering one of the maids or being
heard by Miss Lamb. There was another way out
which she had employed on various occasions. She
opened the window and climbed out into the cold
streaming darkness, wriggled on to the ornamental
stonework over the drawing-room bay, grabbed
the drain-pipe, and made a flurried descent. Then

she began the two-mile journey into Gilding through the December rain, at a half-trot, with panic in her heart.

Mrs. Gateson-Slaughter had made careful preparations for Dawkins' arrival—the distinguishing feature of her carefulness being the care she took to avoid the appearance of care. Her little dining-room was discreetly lighted by shaded candles, so that the dark furniture looked classic and welcoming, there was a noble fire in the grate, and the glasses and table-linen shone in the half-light. Betty was in bed, and the little daily maid, who as a favor had consented to stay for the evening, had been elaborately coached. Gin-and-Italian were awaiting Mr. Dawkins as soon as he had hung up his hat and coat, and Mrs. Gateson-Slaughter laughingly excused herself from joining him in it.

That dinner, regarded as a meal, was a perfect triumph. Mrs. Gateson-Slaughter had been hampered by the need to avoid any appearance of unusual luxury, and also by the untrustworthiness of the maid as a cook, which necessitated her cooking everything herself beforehand and leaving it for the maid to serve. Mrs. Gateson-Slaughter surmounted these difficulties marvelously, and no one would have dreamed who saw her, calm and assured, with opulent bare arms shimmering in the candle-light, that five minutes before Dawkins' arrival she had been enveloped in a coverall heatedly administering the finishing touches to the potatoes.

Oysters came first, that easiest of all dishes to prepare and the most enjoyable to eat. Fine oysters they were, fat and full-flavored, and Dawkins' soul rejoiced in them. The oysters were succeeded by soup, smooth and agreeable and seasoned with the delicacy of true art, and with it a sherry of the better class—just one glassful of liquid sunshine. And Mrs. Gateson-Slaughter talked in her pleasant contralto, while Dawkins expanded and grew less and less reserved, and looked more and more interestedly at that full throat and arms a-gleam across the table against the darkness of the corner of the room. Fricassee of chicken, with aristocratically-mashed potatoes and the most beautiful spinach followed the soup, and Mrs. Gateson-Slaughter, with a vein of seriousness in her light-hearted voice, pressed Dawkins to sample the Burgundy. A wonderful wine it was; it had cost Mrs. Gateson-Slaughter nearly as much as a new frock would have done, but she had looked upon it as money well spent. It was the finest Burgundy the best wine merchant in Gilding could supply, and Mrs. Gateson-Slaughter had aired it with infinite care. It bore within it all the wit of Voltaire, the effectiveness of Maupassant, the exuberance of Borotra, the art of Coquelin, the splendor of Versailles, and the placid joys of the Saône. It warmed and it delighted; it was a heady nectar.

Dawkins sipped and savored and sipped again, and the wine tinged his thoughts with its own roseate hue. The wine was nectar, the chicken ambrosia, and Mrs. Gateson-Slaughter was—Venus? Juno? Some one too delightful for words, anyway. So exquisite was the whole effect that Dawkins wisely declined to cloy his palate with the perfect meringue pudding which appeared, but contented himself with a bite of fine Gruyère cheese and a biscuit. He hardly noticed himself agreeing with Mrs. Gateson-Slaughter's suggestion that he should sample the port—another wine over which Mrs. Gateson-Slaughter had spent some minutes' anxious discussion with the wine merchant. A goodly port, worthy of mention along with the Burgundy, than which there could be no higher praise.

Mrs. Gateson-Slaughter eyed Dawkins' exalted benignancy of expression across the table, and decided that she had reached the effect she had aimed at, so that she made up her mind not to call in the additional aid of the liqueur brandy she held in reserve. She wanted Dawkins to be merely mellow and with a faltering self-control; she did not want him anything like drunk.

And after dinner Mrs. Gateson-Slaughter proposed that they should remain in the cozy dining-room, and Dawkins agreed automatically. He was settled into a comfortable chair at the side of the fire, and Mrs. Gateson-Slaughter sank gracefully on to a low *pouffe* in front of the fire—a well-chosen strategic position, with the firelight on her face and the coffee-table at her feet, for she was just, but not obviously, within Dawkins' reach should he, as Mrs. Gateson-Slaughter fully intended, want to reach toward her.

The conversation had flowed unobtrusively but steadily; Mrs. Gateson-Slaughter had been prettily solicitous about Nina's health and her school record, charmingly interested in the golf handicap, full of tender thought for the garden and the *Baby*, and had harked back with delightful anxiety to the futures of Nina and Betty. This was the subject they began to discuss as the flickering firelight played over Mrs. Gateson-Slaughter's wistful face. They were two such exceptional girls, and they were so happy and friendly together, and Mrs. Gateson-Slaughter thought they were *such* a good influence on each other. In fact she was always heartily sorry on the days when Nina came calling, to separate them at the end of the evening.

And insensibly running alongside this appealing topic there was another one stealing along seemingly unnoticed, whose main theme was the troubles of widows and of Mrs. Gateson-Slaughter in particular. For there ought to be a man in control of every child; she often wished that Betty had a man to look up to, for a man could set an example to his daughter in some ways impossible to a mother. A child was nearly as unfortunate to be fatherless as she was to be motherless—for, of course, after all the mother was the most important influence. There were some matters only a mother could hope to be of any use in. A child who had no woman to whom to take her confidences was—— But Mrs. Gateson-Slaughter never succeeded in saying what she was. She never had the chance of passing on to her final descriptions of the trials and tribulations of this world and how she could hardly bear them longer.

For there was a knock at the door, and the little maid who had been washing up in the kitchen went to open it. They heard a low-voiced argument in the hall, and then the maid looked in.

"Please'm," she said, but she got no further, for somebody else slipped into the room behind her— a little draggled waif of a somebody from whose clothes the water ran in little trickles.

"Nina!" said Dawkins, but no sound came from Mrs. Gateson-Slaughter save a hissing intake of breath.

Nina stood there in the candle-light with her wet hair and her drawn features, and the Hawk's long chin and the Hawk's gray eyes seemed to Dawkins' dazzled gaze to have come back from the grave. It was only with an effort that he tore himself free from the numb bedazement which had settled down upon him, instantly succeeding his previous mood of expansive and admiring sympathy.

"Whatever have you came here for?" asked Dawkins, and it was a second or two before the answer came.

"You—you're wanted back at home," she said—
she had no real idea of what she said.

"Why? Good gracious, is anything wrong?"

Nina nodded silently. Of a sudden she felt very
stupid and tired.

"Whatever is it? Something can't have happened to Miss Lamb?"

Nina shook her head; the water from her clothes
was forming a little puddle round her feet.

"Well, then, what is it? Tell me, Nina."

But Nina still said nothing.

"Tell us at once, you naughty little girl," said
Mrs. Gateson-Slaughter, and all her exasperated
disappointment breathed venomously in every syllable. It was this which roused Dawkins from his
previous rather ordinary mood to one of anxious
receptivity.

"Come on, Nina, old lady," he said. "Let's have
it."

Nina's glance moved from him to Mrs. Gateson-
Slaughter, and met hers like a fencer's with a flash
of parry and ripost, and then moved back again.
The long chin seemed even longer than usual, and
the gray eyes were as hard as stones. Even so did
the Hawk appear at the bad times.

"You've *got* to come home," said Nina, and Dawkins automatically rose from his chair to obey.

In a flash Mrs. Gateson-Slaughter stood barring his path.

"This is all too silly," she said. "Why on earth should you go home just because this child says you must, Mr. Dawkins?"

The three of them stood looking at one another like characters at the climax of some old-fashioned melodrama, but none of them felt at all melodramatic, somehow.

"Come on," said Nina to Dawkins steadily, and Dawkins prepared to obey. He was not obeying Nina, his little girl ward, but the Hawk's daughter, or the Hawk himself, for that matter—it may have been Fate, or it may have been Mrs. Gateson-Slaughter's port, but all remembrance of his resolves never to give way to Nina's whims had vanished, and he remained Nina's humble and devoted servant.

"I think I had better go," he said to Mrs. Gateson-Slaughter, and that lady bit her lip and clenched her hands and would have stamped with rage if she had not restrained herself by a wild effort. As it was she could say nothing.

Dawkins had reached the door before a trace of common sense returned to him.

"By George, old lady. You're wet through. We can't possibly drive you home like that."

They hesitated together before Dawkins turned to Mrs. Gateson-Slaughter.

"Could Nina have some of Betty's things to go home in, do you think?" he asked, and Mrs. Gateson-Slaughter knew not what to reply. To refuse would be churlish; to agree would be to fall in with Mr. Dawkins' project of going home. Her hesitation and the struggle on her face were obvious, and Mrs. Gateson-Slaughter instantly fell several degrees in Dawkins' estimation. Dry clothes after getting wet were one of the points Mr. Dawkins was quite fanatical about, and to hesitate about giving them was a crime in his eyes. His eyebrows came together in a fierce frown, and the terrible gleam appeared in his eyes. He had instantly become Nina's confederate as well as her hereditary retainer, and even Mrs. Gateson-Slaughter quailed before the menace his attitude seemed to convey.

"All right," she said, and she weakly led Nina up-stairs.

Betty, sleeping the sleep of the young and well-plumped, was suddenly roused by the switching on of her bedroom light and the entrance of two people. One seemed to be her mother, who was not such an unusual phenomenon, the other, so her bedazed eyes told her, but she could not credit them, was Nina. Betty promptly imagined herself dreaming, and as in a dream she saw Nina strip herself of her clothes and towel herself with Betty's own towel, while her mother rummaged in her drawers and produced an assortment of Betty's not-too-well-mended underclothing and outer clothing. Betty saw Nina dress herself in these, and then the vision receded and the light went out, leaving Betty quite convinced she had been dreaming. It was only her discovery next morning of Nina's wet clothes which dispelled the idea—and she got small satisfaction from her mother when she asked questions about what had happened.

Down-stairs the front door was open, and Dawkins had his overcoat on and the engine of the car started. Nina came mistily down-stairs and Dawkins wrapped her up in the rugs in the front seat. He looked round to say good-by, but Mrs. Gateson-Slaughter's temper had got the better of her and she had gone in and savagely slammed the front door. Dawkins raised his eyebrows philosophically, and scrambled into the driver's seat. He pushed the gear lever forward, and the car crawled into Gilding High Street, turned the corner and leaped smoothly forward. Dawkins pressed the accelerator, and the car sang through the outskirts of Gilding, seemed to clear instantly, at a bound, the mile of high road, swung neatly into the side lane, swung round the two sharp corners, and came to a halt outside the Other House. Nina was nodding in her seat, and Dawkins carried her in. Miss Lamb met them in the hall and followed them up to Nina's bedroom, and there, without a word, Dawkins handed her over and went down-stairs. He was not in the mood to discuss the business with anybody that night.

CHAPTER XXI

ND the next morning when the realization had crystallized that both his behavior and Nina's had been quite fantastic he felt still worse. For the first time since they had been in the Other House he came down late to breakfast, deliberately, because he felt shy of encountering Nina, and after breakfast he haled Miss Lamb into his study and put her through a savage cross-examination, because he was exceedingly savage. He demanded to know the why and the wherefore, how Nina had got out of the house without Miss Lamb's knowledge, and what the dickens Miss Lamb meant by allowing the child to go out for a two-mile walk in December rain, and what had put the idea into Nina's head anyway.

Miss Lamb, despite the fact that all her newfound happiness was at stake, received the storm with unbowed head like the patrician she was. Yes, she had told Nina that he was dining at Mrs. Gateson-Slaughter's. That was because Nina had asked when she had taken in her supper. She had said nothing else on the subject. Yes, it was her fault that Nina had got out of the house. She was fully responsible, and was guilty of inattention to duty in allowing it. She had come to the conclusion that Nina had got out of the window and down the drain-pipe via the cornice. Yes, it would be dangerous, especially in the dark, but not so very dangerous to an active little girl. She had no idea why Nina had suddenly decided to go to Mrs. Gateson-Slaughter's unless—— Unless? Unless—perhaps—Nina had felt jealous of the lady for some reason or other. She did not know what had happened at Mrs. Gateson-Slaughter's, but she hoped it had been nothing unpleasant.

Dawkins raged again, guiltily, and dropped the subject. For the rest of the day he cursed himself for his timidity toward Nina. He decided several times for and against running into Gilding and apologizing to Mrs. Gateson-Slaughter—and did not go. The whole afternoon he spent screwing up his courage to tackle Nina on her return from school. It took quite a lot of courage on his part. He heard Nina come in from school. He heard her go in to tea with Miss Lamb. He waited half an hour and then he rang the bell and told Mary to "ask Miss Nina to come and speak to me before she starts her home work."

Nina came, and of course her gray eyes and her long chin came with her, and Dawkins with set face waved her into the opposite armchair. Dawkins had tried to rehearse an opening, but he had been hampered by the quite remakably acute realization of the necessity not to vent upon Nina the rage he felt with himself.

"I want to hear all about what you did last night," he said, keeping his voice desperately even, "and why you did it."

But Nina refused to be overawed by his judicial attitude and refused to subside into the ordinary Nina. She remained the Nina of the transcendent personality of last night.

"You know what I did," she said. "I got out of the window and came and fetched you home. And you ought to know why I did it."

Dawkins, uneasily, did know, and that was what was embarrassing him. But he stuck to his guns.

"Don't you know," he said, "that it was very naughty of you to get up after you went to bed, and to sneak out of the house without letting Miss

Lamb know? And you might have hurt yourself
very badly climbing down that drain-pipe, and you
might easily have caught pneumonia or something
very bad like that if Mrs. Gateson-Slaughter hadn't
been so kind as to lend you some of Betty's
clothes?"

Nina's only reply was a sneer.

"Mrs. Gateson-Slaughter!" she said, and every
syllable was quick with contempt.

"Yes, Mrs. Gateson-Slaughter," said Dawkins,
clinging wildly to the offensive. "She is a very nice
lady, and was much nicer to you than you deserve."

Nina thumped the arm of her chair and threw
away all vestige of a tolerant hearing of Dawkins' remarks.

"Oh, it's silly to talk like that, daddy," she said.
"You know she wasn't and isn't and won't be ever.
You *do* know that."

Gray eyes met blue eyes on terms of equality and
climbed speedily to superiority.

"She isn't any good at all," said Nina, and her
voice gradually assumed a far more maternal tone
even than the one she used toward Betty.

"You know, she isn't a bit like what you think
she is. She thinks camping and that sort of thing

is all rot, like our going exploring on the *Baby*. *She* doesn't want to go up the Amazon or the Orinoco. And she hates me—oh, she does. It'd be awful if you married her."

"But——"

"Oh, I know she wants to marry you. She told Betty so, but I'd have known even if Betty hadn't told me."

Dawkins gaped at Nina wordlessly. All sorts of illusions were crashing round him—most of them had already been undermined, and these disclosures by Nina brought them down with a run. That Mrs. Gateson-Slaughter should want to marry him reduced her value in Dawkins' eyes enormously. Dawkins was that sort of man, and he was old-fashioned enough to consider it unwomanly for a woman to want to marry any one, to say nothing of attempting to bring it about. From that very moment Mrs. Gateson-Slaughter ceased in his eyes to be a desirable, almost unattainable goddess and lapsed into some one to be run away from. Nina with her devilish intuition was aware of the fact.

A very curious, rather comforting atmosphere suddenly grew up between the two of them, and Nina unconsciously added to it by slipping out of her chair and climbing up on to Dawkins' knee. She punched him in the chest and looked into his eyes. With every gesture she proclaimed that she was still only a child, but at the same time there was something about her appearance and about Dawkins' attitude which took her sex and her sexual ascendency over Dawkins for granted.

"I'm glad you're not going to marry her," said Nina. "I wouldn't like you to marry even the nicest woman in the world."

She eyed Dawkins with the expression of some one hesitating to impart some new revelation. And Dawkins' blue eyes smiled back at her. He was feeling incredibly happy with this warm bundle in his arms. He seemed suddenly to have come out of some fantastic and badly lighted world into a world of solidity and light. The smile in Dawkins' eyes was more than Nina could resist.

"You know why, don't you?" she said. "It isn't because of the French rivers or the Amazon or the Orinoco or anything like that."

And she leaned forward to him, and Dawkins felt on his mustached mouth the touch of her lips, warm and friendly and childlike. Then they looked at each other, joint sharers in a great secret.

CHAPTER XXII

SO ALL that winter and the next spring Dawkins' life and Nina's, too, moved along ordinary lines. Dawkins did his work at the settlement in his thorough fashion, still feeling oddly out of his element, but earning the devotion and the regard of all those who saw the value of the work he did. He put his hand in his pocket for the sake of the charities that were administered under his eye; he collected facts and information; he took parties of mothers to the seaside. Now and again a gust of passion would take him by the throat and he would not reach home until the next day, but that was only to be expected. Miss Lamb, in fact, with surprising shrewdness, became accustomed to these periodic absences, and one can hardly help suspecting that she guessed the reason for them. It is even to be feared that little Miss Lamb, virtuous Miss Lamb, maidenly Miss Lamb, condoned them in her heart, and sought and found excuses for her hero.

The golf made steady, automatic, almost inevitable progress. Dawkins' handicap came down by occasional ones or even twos. Membership in the Manor Club came to him without a struggle, and there Dawkins was able to hobnob with wealth and blue blood and to drift into desired but unsought popularity. He was helped in that, indeed, by his acquaintance with one of the most eminent members of all the Gilding Manor Club—a very Eminent Gentleman indeed, who twinkled at him in the dining-room on his first visit and asked how the exploring was getting on, and played a round with him in the afternoon, and returned full of admiration at an exhibition of immense driving and iron nerve. But nobody in the club ever guessed that the reason why Dawkins was so modest and retiring about the exposure of his person in the wash-room after a round on a wet day was because his back was seamed with crisscross scars acquired in a South American convict prison.

The rumors which associated him with monstrous wealth gradually died away after he had disposed of all his jewels and had comfortably invested the proceeds. Mr. Carver had stolen very little from him, thanks to Dawkins' minute examination of accounts and his consistency in handing over small parcels at a time. Carver had privately decided that he would inveigle all the remaining stones from Dawkins in one large batch and then simply keep them and defy Dawkins to prosecute him to regain possession. But he had no opportunity—in fact he did not know that the supply had come to an end until he had sold the last of them. However, Carver had made something over a comfortable fifty thousand pounds and had no real grounds for complaint; and Dawkins could draw rather more than four thousand pounds a year from his gilt-edged investments. It was more than he needed for everything he wanted to do, so that he was far richer than most people in the world. The feeling of respectability and permanence was most astonishingly comfortable, and his love for Nina and her little tender affection for him kept him happy.

Nina did not say anything more to him during those months about the secret they shared, of course. No child would. In fact any casual observer might imagine that it was quite forgotten, for Nina went on in her own child's way, with occasional little tempers and occasional naughti-

nesses, wriggling from one trouble to another at
school, although it was not for a long time that she
came into contact with authority as violently as the
time when she was "liable to expulsion." Home
work and hockey and riding lessons, and tennis
when the summer came round; any unthinking person would have decided on observation that these
things bulked far more importantly in Nina's life
than Dawkins did—but whoever thought so would
have been wrong.

Summer brought other things besides tennis.
There were week-end trips in the *Baby*, and despite all the imminent preparations for the Con-
tinental voyage, and despite the fact that they had
explored the Thames so thoroughly the previous
summer, they were periods of sheer delight to
which Dawkins, Nina and Miss Lamb looked forward one and all. The other girls at Gilding High
School listened enviously to Nina's accounts of
the forty-eight-hour Odysseys, and they most heartily envied Nina the possession of such a wonderful
guardian as she had. They had seen him sometimes at hockey matches and on Sports Day, big,
blond and terrible, and yet deliciously human—
and did he not sometimes cook sausages over an oil

stove, which not one in a hundred of their own respectable something-in-the-City fathers would ever have dreamed of doing? Dawkins hardly knew it, but he was an object of worship to quite three hundred bits of femininity in Gilding, to say nothing of the mothers who admired from afar. But Nina knew it, and the knowledge gave her an unreasoning but wholly satisfactory pride. The memory of an ingeniously ill-tempered auntie, and of something not quite respectable at home which had made her the object of the derision of her schoolmates at private school, was being overlaid and erased with comforting rapidity.

Nina did not know of one period of mortal terror through which Dawkins had passed, and she would have been frantic with fear if she had known about it. For letters had come to Dawkins, addressed to him in care of the first branch of the National County bank which he had patronized. They had come from auntie, and they were speciously worded demands for the return of Nina to her. Dawkins had sweated with terror when the first one came, but he had held himself free from panic. Dreading the least bit of scandal which might deprive Nina of her new-found respectability he had hurried to London (he would not chance the leakage of gossip from a Gilding lawyer) and had put himself unreservedly in the hands of the best firm of solicitors to whom the Eminent Gentleman could recommend him. They had hummed and hawed, and had raised amazed eyebrows at the sight of the would-be legal document which Mrs. Royle had signed on his first taking Nina away, but they assured him in the end that if he was on the wrong side of the law Mrs. Royle was also, and finally they had dealt with Mrs. Royle in such a fashion that at long last, and at the cost of a few more hundreds, Dawkins found himself constituted legal guardian of Nina with formalities which not even the Lord Chancellor could controvert.

This end was only reached, however, when summer was fairly come, and Nina would not have been much interested in the business even if Dawkins had told her about it, for there were such heaps of other excitements to distract her. Her year in the fourth form had passed like a flash, and was ending now in a splutter of examinations, and Nina was beginning to consider the possibility of finding herself next year in the fifth form, a height which made even the Everest-summit of the sixth seemingly attainable. But school work faded into unimportance when the imminence of the French tour came into Nina's mind. Mr. Dawkins was busy having the *Baby* registered, and obtaining *permis de voyage,* and attending to the half-hundred details necessary to insure unrestricted access to the interior of France. Crises in the correspondence occurred weekly, and the breakfast-table atmosphere at the Other House alternated between elation and depression with the variations of the mind of French officialdom.

Miss Lamb quite began to put on airs, because the correspondence in French was necessarily carried on by her. Yet even Miss Lamb was not infallible, and came a nasty cropper in one of the letters wherein she had to transpose the *Baby's* draught of water from feet to meters—for she was guilty of a mistake in arithmetic for which she would have censured Nina with all the mild severity of which she was capable. And the arguments she had with Dawkins about the exact meanings of *flottable* and *navigable!* It was all too exciting for words.

Yet it all came about. As soon as ever the summer term was finished they were on board the

Baby with the paid hand they had engaged for the run across, and they nosed their way amid hectic incidents through London and down the Pool and out past the North Foreland. They waited their chance for a favorable day, and ran across the Straits, so that Nina's delighted eyes rested for the first time on the coast of France. Then they crawled onward past all the seaside resorts in the full swing of the bourgeois August season, and crept past Havre into the wide green estuary of the Seine.

Nina would not have liked to have to state which she preferred, the open sea or the rivers; both had so much to be said in their favor. The sea was wide and exciting (Nina was never seasick— not like poor Miss Lamb, who would have stated her preference in no uncertain terms), and the *Baby's* engine could be opened full out. But rivers were her first love, after all, and the green fields seen through gray rain, and the strange chalky cliffs of the lower Seine, and the immense turns and twists of the river made her heart beat faster and brought a queer little lump into her throat. There was enormous excitement, too, in going shopping with Miss Lamb, and her respect for that lady was vastly enhanced by the ease with which she conversed with village folk. The French of the Gilding High School, Nina found, was not much use in a motor-boat on the Seine—and even daddy, the invincible, was quite hopeless even in such a simple matter as asking the way.

Then there was Jumieges Abbey, too, and St. Wandrille and Caudebec, and then Rouen, and a perfectly astonishing climb *inside* the walls of Rouen Cathedral up to where you looked down from such a height that you experienced an odd sensation as if a big hand had gripped your stomach and were squeezing it. Then the non-tidal Seine, with its green hills which were so hospitable and friendly, as though they were little cousins of Summer Hill far back at the Other House, and the pleasant fields of Normandy, until factory buildings began to grow more and more frequent, and the reaches of the river shorter and shorter, and Paris was at hand and the Eiffel Tower plain to see.

Perhaps the passage through Paris gave Nina a rather distorted idea of geography. Paris for her was not the Queen of Europe, nor the burial place of Napoleon; she was not even now quite old enough to look on it as the place that frocks come from. Instead, Nina came to look upon Paris as a nasty place covering the river for thirty long kilometers without a single suitable spot to tie up in, which from fear of delays they entered into at dawn and pushed hurriedly through all day. The St. Denis canal enabled them to cut off the corner between La Briche and the Île du Cité, but it involved a horrible, smoky, gloomy, sickly journey through tunnels and along commercial waterways at their worst. Nina simply hated Paris, and was not a bit pleased when Miss Lamb promised that she would bring her there again at Christmas by a more normal route, so that they could see Notre Dame and the Louvre and the shops without being bothered about tieing-up places.

But it was worth all the fatigue and squalor of the passage through Paris when once they had won their way through and the *Baby* began to chug her way through the clear water of the upper Seine alongside the beautiful woods of Fontainebleau, with Barbizon close to the river, where Miss Lamb talked sentimentally about Trilby. And the wooded banks of Fontainebleau were succeeded by the steep valley of the Yonne, and every day, wet or fine, clouded or sunny, was a miracle of beauty and peace, and every night was one of friendly good-fellowship, so that Nina came to love the sound of the quiet breathing of Miss Lamb in the other berth when she woke in the night, and reveled in the knowledge that Dawkins was sleeping under his green canvas awning just outside the cabin door. Every minute of that time Nina was thrilled with the realization of what a wonderful holiday she was having.

They left the Yonne at Laroche and began the wonderful climb up the Burgundy Canal, rising higher and higher with each lock passed through. Nina came to realize that a canal can be every bit as exciting as a river, because a river necessarily flows in a valley, while a really sensible canal, like this one of Burgundy, will pass clear over hilltops. There is something marvelous about steering one's boat over the roof of the world, as Nina did while they passed the terraced vineyards of Burgundy.

It could not last for ever, of course, as even Nina admitted. They made the dark and weird passage of the Pouilly tunnel with the aid of a pilot, and then they dropped down again, lock by lock, flight after flight of locks, through Dijon to the placid sober meanderings of the Saône. And yet those placid undetermined reaches of river, running through green meadowland, were strangely satisfactory, too. Their very ordinariness was a merit after the Homeric perfection of the Burgundy Canal. Châlon, as Nina saw regretfully on the map, was their "farthest South"; it was not for them to penetrate this year through to the Rhone and the Mediterranean. They turned aside with hearts full of sadness into the busy commerce of the Canal du Centre, hurried through the commercialized district centering on Le Creusot, and in due course made a sedate arrival upon the Loire.

But the Loire was not for them; the *Baby* drew too much water for that treacherous stream with its shifting sandbanks and summer shallows. They were confined to the more prosaic water of the Lateral Canal, but Nina and Miss Lamb and Dawkins were quite satisfied even with that, and they cruised on past Digoin and Nevers and Sancerre and Cosne, while the guide-books foamed at the mouth with superlatives regarding the history of the castles and abbeys they left at every kilometer. And then almost before they realized it they were back on the Seine again at Fontainebleau, with Paris close ahead of them. That was the end of the most perfect and wonderful six weeks Nina could ever remember, for holidays were nearly over, and Nina and Miss Lamb had to leave Dawkins to take the *Baby* single-handed down to Rouen, there to find paid hands to assist in the navigation back to England.

Not even the magic of the train and steamer could dim the luster of the memory of that voyage. At every half-hour of the journey Nina remembered some incident to chatter about to Miss Lamb: the collision with the barge at Suresnes, the time when Miss Lamb had to buy a spark-plug from a seemingly idiotic motor-accessory dealer at Dijon, and the historic occasion near Nevers when a drifting bit of rope twined itself round the propeller shaft, so that Dawkins had to hang head-downward over the stern with a wildly agitated Miss Lamb and a hysterical Nina holding on to his legs while he disentangled the frightful mess.

Nina was most desperately determined, by the time they reached home again, that next year would find them pushing for the Black Sea via the Rhine and the Danube, and that the year after that they would be on the Nile or the Volga. She regretted hourly the years that must pass before she was sixteen—that being the age limit she had set herself, without consulting either Dawkins or Miss Lamb, for remaining at Gilding High School before setting out for the Amazon and the Orinoco, real rivers, unmapped, untraveled, with the additional attractions of savage animals, hostile tribes and doubtful food supply.

In fact she was far more interested in the Rhine and the Danube than in the first stages of womanhood through which Miss Lamb was anxiously piloting her; these last were inevitable, and, to Nina, not very important. She did not realize what a change had suddenly come about in herself, although it was a huge surprise to Dawkins when he rejoined them after a fortnight's absence. Much of the change had, indeed, occurred in that fortnight, the rest had passed unnoticed somehow during the French voyage and only dawned upon Dawkins, all at once, on his return.

Instead of the rather fragile child he was expecting to see, Dawkins saw, with a shock, that Nina was now an opening bud of womanhood. There was something a little different in the eyes and face—not much, and Nina would not have liked it had she been told so, but an undoubted change. And blending with the dainty boyish figure there was a suspicion, more than a slight suspicion, of bosom and hips. The little piquant change wrung Dawkins' very vitals. He hated it and was charmed with it and was unsettled by it and tried to reconcile himself to it all in the same instant. It was change, and by this time Dawkins' chief desire was stability. He dreaded what it portended, even while he could not perceive any alteration at all in Nina's manner toward him and the rest of the world. He hated himself for the discovery that a man comes to love a budding woman in a different way from the way he loves a child. There were moments when he could not keep from his mind vague visualizations of the slight tender breasts beneath the white drill blouse, and he spurned himself savagely for visualizing them. He was like a monk in his desperate battling with the flesh.

The time might come when he could settle down to the new conditions, when he could accustom himself to Platonic, parental affection. But that time was not yet—not while the features of the Hawk, whom he had loved, and of the child-Nina whom he had loved, blended with those of the woman-Nina whom he grew instantly to love.

And that is the end of this story, for the rest of the history of Nina and of Dawkins has not yet been achieved. For Nina is still in the fifth form of Gilding High School for Girls and is still poring over maps of the Danube in preparation for next summer's voyage, and Dawkins still spends successive days at the Manor Golf Club and Gilding Golf Club, trying to reduce his handicap from six to five, and at Mr. Gray's East End Settlement trying to act as though charitable actions are natural to him.

We can not pry into the future, and if we could we would hardly dare to do so, for Dawkins' future seems gray and sad and depressing however we examine it. We can only be sure of one thing: that Dawkins will be ready to make any sacrifice for Nina's sake, and it seems as if that stern common sense of his will make the sacrifice pitifully severe. Maybe that stern common sense of his will keep him from marrying Nina and so courting disaster—a marriage of nearing fifty to nearing twenty, for doubtless Nina, before she has time to look much about her and to arrange her thoughts in mature fashion will be willing enough to marry her dear daddy should he ask her. There is even the faint comforting hope that the marriage should it take place would not be disastrous; that Dawkins' tender loving-kindness and sound instinct would hold it together during the years which lie between fifty and senility.

And yet we can not bring ourselves to believe in this marriage; Dawkins is far too ready to sacrifice himself for Nina. He will hold back until the twenties come, and he will watch the young men come sidling round Nina—polished, moneyed young men who will call him "sir" and pay only the vaguest attention to him, poor old dodderer, while their eyes continually stray aside to Nina, and the inevitable moment will arise when Nina will cast aside her poor old daddy as heartlessly as any young woman in love ever does. Dawkins' keen blue eyes, faded a little now, perhaps, will run minutely over the young man without his being aware of it, and will weigh him up, and he will decide that he is almost good enough for Nina. Then Dawkins will come down with a handsome settlement and his blessing, and Nina will leave him, almost without a thought, to the blue devils of loneliness and regret. He has never merited whatever good fortune has come to him, anyway.

THE END

2/23

25
19   3/23